# Almost

Deena C. Miller Wingard

ISBN 978-1-960853-11-0

Liberation's Publishing – West Point, MS.

# Acknowledgement

I began drafting this book in 2006 when I was experiencing many of the stressors Balynda does. As a writer of poetry in my youth, I dreamed of becoming a published author. Instead, it was during the height of my life stressors, I found solace and therapy in my writing. My desire is that this book brings comfort and clarity to the lives of many. The completion of it has not gone without pain, distractions, and setbacks. These events are my confirmation that the enemy knows the freeing power that will be released to many after reading *Almost*. It has little to do with me, as I was just willing and obedient enough to write it. It has everything to do with walking in God's will. I am simply a vessel.

When I moved to Atlanta from Cleveland, Ohio, in 2003, it seemed like all hell broke loose in my life. I often questioned God and wondered why He led me to come to Atlanta. God later revealed that the issues were always there; I had just swept them under the rug. I also surmised that I came to Atlanta to join Voices of Faith Church. The teaching and guidance of Bishop Gary Hawkins, Sr., propelled my spiritual walk and calling to another plane. The Voices of Faith Church Family has been my rock. I love you eternally. Thank you for the support, love, and friendship over the years.

I met my husband, Elgin L. Wingard, when my life was on

the upswing in 2012. I had just received a promotion at work and a spiritual promotion as an ordained church elder. I was also a student at McAfee School of Theology when we met, raising my minor children. Despite my busy schedule, he came into my life and brought more stability and excitement. Elgin, you endure my working way into the night and early in the morning daily, and for that, I am grateful. It is not easy being married to me, but I hope it is worth the ride.

As I look back upon the start of this book, I think about the beta reader of my first chapter, Ron Barnes. He joked that *I must be under a lot of stress* after reading my first draft. However, his humor, friendship, and support helped me through that challenging time. Ron, thank you for being a faithful friend.

Thank you to my editor and friend, Sharahnne Gibbons, and my beta reader and friend, Mrs. Brenda Walker. I received some wounds while completing this book, and you both helped me heal.

To my church that God directed me to establish and pastor, Shekinah Greater Love Tabernacle, Inc., thank you for trusting the God in me. Whether you are an active, or inactive, current, or past member, I love you from the bottom of my heart. I also honor our many supporters and friends who may have church membership elsewhere, yet you continuously cheer us on. God has a blessing with your name on it.

I also want to thank the following people for being my

friends to whom I can confide and be myself: Carlotta Warner, Camille Gregory, David Gregory, Pastor Cheri Harris, Pastor Carlos Marshall, Deborah Asbury, Felicia Brooks Williams, Delloyd Wilson, Roy Brown, William Franklin, Herbert Spencer, Dr. Deatra L. Neal, Naomi Duncan, Nicanor Smith, Annette Smith, Bernadette Dennis, Sonya Chapman, Carla Hunter, and Dr. Chavonne Stewart. You are my chosen family.

To the late Bishop Alfred L. Ringer, life is not the same without you. You were always my biggest cheerleader, and I know you are cheering for me now in heaven.

I acknowledge my ministry and business professionals who have become my dear friends: Jermaine Foster, Michael Foreman, and Sherry Nwosu. My calling is more attainable because of you.

I extend a special note of gratitude to my Life Coach, Dr. Jamie Cross-Lee. You help me get past all the distractions and noise to see what God is saying and doing. Thank you for helping me stay laser focused.

To my father, Dr. Elder Robert L. Lewis, thank you for your sacrifices for our family. I had the opportunity to care for you when I was completing this book. You were the best company for our trips to Barnes & Noble. You would allow me to write uninterrupted while you perused all the books. You were like a kid in a candy store! Thank you for instilling in me the love of reading and teaching me the importance of being a lifelong learner.

My resiliency and grit came from and are exemplified by my mother, Laura J. Lewis McDole. Thank you, Mema, for teaching my sister Valerie J. Lewis Coleman and me how to keep on keeping on.

I am grateful for my bonus offspring: Elgin Wingard II, Emanuel Wingard, and Jocelyn Wingard. Let us continue to increase our bond. The best is yet to be.

I conclude by letting my babies know I would move the world for you all. I am sure you already know that, yet I realize I am far from a perfect mother. Nonetheless, your mother loves you beyond measure: Aisha Hardaway, Marcus Miller, and Charisse Miller.

To my first babies: my nephews Lamarr and LaShawn Lewis; you two have grown into the most amazing young men. Thank you and your beautiful families for loving me as well.

Above all, thank You, God, for constantly downloading into me what You desire I share with the world. May I always be pleasing in Your sight.

I had fainted, unless I had believed to see the goodness of the LORD in the land of the living.

Psalm 27:13

Deena C. Miller Wingard

# Table of Contents

# ❧ Chapter One

In the winter of February 2016, the Cleveland Police Department tactical crew took position outside the apartment door. Even though it was early in the morning, many neighbors began to peek out their windows in hopes of catching a glimpse of some excitement. Unfortunately, the once-thriving neighborhood had taken a drastic decline over the years and now seemed only to harbor those up to no good.

Balynda's heart pounded as she waited for the count. She quickly moved her freshly pressed hair off her forehead to avoid contact with the beads of nervous perspiration that had begun to accumulate despite the cool temperature. As a social worker, Balynda had participated in several removals, but this one was different. The parents were both known around the neighborhood for their raging tempers and erratic behavior.

"One," the lead police officer whispered as he extended his index finger in the air.

He then broke the intense silence as he stated, "Two."

Balynda pressed against the plastered wall. Her chest heaved as paint chips fluttered onto her shoulders.

"Three!"

The lead man kicked open the door. Three armed officers rushed inside the apartment. Assessing the environment, they observed two half-dressed adults on the couch, a pile of some type of debris, and a chipped cocktail table slightly tilting to the left. On the chipped table, sat a couple of empty liquor bottles and a 9mm handgun.

The startled boyfriend jumped off the couch. He grabbed the gun on the table and wielded it in the air. "What the ---"

Two officers tackled him to the floor, kicked the gun away, and then restrained him. Two more officers entered the home. One of them grabbed the gun that had slid under the table. The team searched the furniture-sparse apartment for firearms, drugs, and money. Barely cognizant of what was transpiring, an intoxicated woman attempted to get off the couch to confront the home invaders. Instead, she fell back on the couch, spewed vulgarities, and slumped in an apparent state of stupor. Then, two screaming children ran from the back room without pause, tears streaming down their chubby faces.

"Clear!" the lead man nodded at Balynda.

Balynda wiped the sweat that dripped from her palms on her khakis and moved toward the children. She stumbled over the pile of debris that she now recognized as a mountain of soiled diapers, dirty clothes, and food remnants. Maintaining her balance, she swooped the toddler in her left arm and used her right hip to direct the second child to the door.

"It's okay, babies. We're going to get you to a safe place." Unfortunately, her attempts to soothe the children did little to calm her own fears.

The one-year-old girl reached for her mother as if trying to grasp a life raft. Her older brother was more concerned with the ensuing wrestling match than with Balynda's efforts to get him out of the apartment. She grabbed his hand to expedite the escape and snatched a stuffed teddy bear off the trash heap on her way out the door.

"Another successful extraction," the lead man said as he escorted the handcuffed man down the outside walkway toward the police cruiser. "Good job, Brown." He brushed the paint chips off her lined wool blazer.

Balynda managed to muster a half-smile for the officer. While she was undoubtedly grateful the children were now safe; she was less able to handle the stress of removals. The anxiety of the unknown was becoming too much for her. "I seriously need a new job," Balynda mumbled.

~ ~ ~ ~ ~

Balynda stared out the picture window of her bedroom later that evening. Safely home, she found the same snow that gave her trepidation on the drive, now mesmerized as it fell freshly to the ground. Winters in Cleveland were no joke. From October to about May, Balynda hibernated whenever possible to minimize her interaction with the blistering cold.

The effect from Lake Erie was known to cause snowfalls over two feet high and routine blizzards. Routine, in that businesses and schools ran as usual despite the inclement weather. Balynda didn't realize how good she had it back in South Carolina. Columbia never experienced this type of treacherous weather. Just the mention of snow sent folks into panic mode and launched the mad rush to grocery stores and The Home Depot.

"Why in the world did I move to this gloomy city in the first place?" Balynda wondered aloud. Oh yes, Zeke, she remembered. After getting her master's degree in social work, her next goal was to get a husband. Her thoughts turned to how she could have aspired to earn a doctorate, start a community center, or even a fitness business. But no, she just had to set her focus on getting married.

Balynda and Zeke dated on and off during high school and kept in touch during their college years. Although they often referred to each other as high school sweethearts, Balynda knew she was one of Zeke's many girlfriends. Their relationship took on new life when they both graduated from separate colleges and began working in downtown Columbia. Zeke professed to have settled down and easily resolidified his place in Balynda's life. Zeke was the first to have captured her heart and it didn't take much for her to fall for his charm again.

Just two weeks after Balynda and Zeke became engaged, he was offered a lucrative position with an architectural firm. She took a stand and refused to move as only his fiancé, so they married. Out of excuses not to move, she followed her man.

A man who finds a wife finds a good thing. "If only I had sat back and let God do His thing," Balynda agonized. She reflected on how she just had to help God out and speed things along. "I guess I just fell victim to the little-girls-must-grow-up-and-get-married mentality," she muttered.

It is not like she *hated* being married. On the contrary, she believed that marriage was a beautiful institution. She got all choked up just reading fairy tales to her daughter, May.

Take *The Little Mermaid*, for example. Ariel gave up the vast ocean, her family, and even her fin just to be with her man. Her sacrifice was not for naught because Eric loved her intensely. When they finally defeated all the naysayers and obstacles, and then embraced in a deep kiss, you could just feel the love pouring from the pages or big screen.

The story made you think about how wonderful it must be to love someone so deeply and have them love you back just as much. Balynda had given up on fairy tales and true love. Unfortunately, the bond joining man and woman together forever no longer seemed prevalent nowadays. She accepted the fact that her marriage "sucked," as she often characterized it. "No sense trying to sugarcoat it," she repeatedly stated, "It is what it is."

She stepped away from the frosty glass. Balynda grabbed the iron and ironing board from the linen closet and ironed the kids' clothes for the next day. She found her nightly chore to also be therapeutic as she tried to iron each wrinkle in the clothes and in her life with every stroke. Her mind scattered through the pages of her life. She replayed her life from thoughts of the gloomy city to the pains of her dreary marriage. Oh, and how could she forget to despair about her dismal job?

*"Okaay!"* She groaned to herself and shook her head to clear the fog. "I'm just going to have a pity party tonight." She removed the iron just before she scorched the sweater. "No sense pretending to enjoy my present circumstances."

"Mama!" Balynda's ten-year-old, May, disrupted the party. "I need some glue for my project."

"When is your project due?

"Tomorrow!"

"Call your daddy. He can bring some home whenever he gets in."

Balynda bit her bottom lip to keep her negative comments to

herself. Her husband had been working late every day for over a month. If she didn't get anything else out of this marriage, she had her beautiful children and the acquired ability to read the signs of infidelity. She wanted to tell her adolescent, "Call your philandering daddy and see if he can pull himself away from his side chick long enough to help a sistah out around this camp!" But, instead, she opted to spare her child from the ongoing adult drama. She promised herself when May was born to teach her to value herself and not to accept poor treatment from her mate. Even though she, herself, did not have the ideal marriage, Balynda wanted her daughter to know she had options, but settling was not one of them.

A few minutes later, May yelled down the stairs. "He said, 'Okay.'"

"Cool," Balynda responded and then returned to ironing. "At least I don't have to go out and face the bitter cold and nine inches of snow."

*Too much!* Balynda ruminated about the blizzard that just ravished much of the Northeast and Mid-Atlantic States, impacting over 100 million people.

*Now that was a disaster! I better just be grateful and count my blessings.* She put her index finger to her mouth, considering the root of her dissatisfaction. *Perhaps I lack a little vitamin D. Nothing a trip to a sunny destination cannot cure*, Balynda fantasized.

~ ~ ~ ~ ~

Balynda finally managed to get the kids ready for bed. No glue yet, so the final touches on the project would have to wait until the morning. May noted she could finish it during Extended Learning Time, so that worked for Balynda. Desmond, her fifteen-year-old son, tried to act as if he no longer desired their standard goodnight kiss and hug ritual. Balynda knew that ten and fifteen-year-olds still yearned to be kissed goodnight and maybe even tucked in, but her energy level was at zero tonight.

Balynda quickly dismissed concerns about tucking in the kids and imagined how wonderful it would feel to be escorted to bed herself. Then finally, she dragged herself to bed intending to get back up to brush her teeth and wash her face. She could hear that the kids were still up and about way past their bedtimes, but Balynda's only pulling force was her mattress. Rather than calling Frances, her best friend, as was their typical nightly routine, she texted her and told her they could chat tomorrow.

It was 3:00 a.m. when Balynda finally knocked off her exhaustion. She had fallen into a deep sleep but was unable to completely rest until she knew her family was safe at home. She patted the area to her left in her king-sized bed. No husband. She popped up and started thinking the worst. What if something terrible really did happen? What if he got in a car accident and was near death in a hospital bed somewhere? Should she start calling the police department to see if anyone reported an accident? Balynda called his cell phone, but Zeke did not pick up.

About ten minutes later, just before she went into full detective mode, she heard the garage door opening. She pretended to be asleep to see what she could find out on the sly. Zeke crept into the room, hoping that she was fast asleep. Balynda heard him in the bathroom going through what she described as his nightly anal-retentive routine. He gave her no clues, other than the fact that it was 3:20 a.m. and he was just getting in from "work."

*To heck, with all the working he is doing*, Balynda said to herself, *I should be able to leave my gloomy job.*

Zeke bowed down on his knees to say his prayers, as he did every night. Although she was used to this ritual, Balynda's mind began to race again. She wondered if he was repenting for his escapades that evening. At least he was still a praying man, she rationalized. Perhaps she was just making a big deal out of nothing. Zeke slid under the covers and offered Balynda no hug, no holding, no nothing. He just turned his back on her and fell asleep. It felt like he had taken a sledgehammer to her already breaking heart. It was as though she could physically feel the cracks emerging as she rocked herself to sleep. She had played in this scene so many times before during their fifteen-year marriage. The strange thing was that it just got harder and harder.

A tear rolled down her cheek as she tried to ignore the

growing lump in her throat. *Well, at least he is home*, she reasoned before finally drifting to sleep.

# ❧ Chapter Two

Balynda tried her best to avoid making eye contact with Zeke the following morning. As she brushed her teeth; she averted her eyes from the mirror for fear of locking gazes with Zeke. It was clear, however, that he was trying his best to determine her headspace. The more Balynda looked away from Zeke, the more he seemed to try to get her attention. Finally, when he could not take the passive cold shoulder anymore, he exclaimed, "Well, good morning to you, Balynda."

"Good morning," she muttered, still wanting to avoid further conversation. Balynda had learned that too much talk always led to a full-blown argument when the tension was this high. She put on the last of her make-up and called out, "Desmond, May, get a move on it!"

Zeke used miniature clippers to trim his baby-soft beard. "So, snatching any kids from their families today?"

Balynda took a long sigh and prepared for battle. "I try not to look at it that way, thank you. Apparently, you don't know by now, but I am in the business of saving children. If that means removing them from abusive and destructive homes, then that is exactly what I will do." She pursed her lips, "By any means necessary."

"Relax, girl! Why are you so feisty? I know you are not tripping about me working late. You know you need to count your blessings! You don't ever have to worry about the bills being pa--"

"Oh, just stop it, Zeke! You are forever trying to deflect from the real issue! I know you weren't working late last night. You were with her again, and we both know it!" She felt the fury rising in her belly. She took three deep breaths to stifle the pending eruption she had tried so fervently to avoid.

"Yeah, right," Zeke's calm, cool tone would have been convincing had her intuition not been triggered. "I told you that is a figment of your imagination. You are just speculating per usual."

"Speculating? So, the fact that you two were seen having intimate lunches and are virtually inseparable at work is speculating?"

"Whatever, Balynda." He slathered on Cartier cologne. "Step to me when you get some real facts. In the meantime, let a brother work in peace." As he walked away, he attempted to sing Bobby Womack's "If You Think You're Lonely Now".

"Well, it's not like you haven't been busted before! I don't care how much you deny it! I know you. Cheating is what you do!"

He turned and looked directly into her eyes. "Leave then. If I am so bad, nothing but a cheater, then why are you still here?" His response caught her by surprise, and she could not think of a clever comeback. Instead, she just looked at him and wondered how they got to this place. How can you go from being the center of someone's world to them no longer wanting you in their world? As Zeke left the room, she could hear the kids running down the steps to grab a quick Breakfast. Letting out another exasperating sigh, she agonized *Here I go again having to go to work with a heavy heart and mind. I'm so tired of feeling so boxed in and burdened.*

"Why am I still here?" She said aloud, mocking Zeke's question. Then seriously contemplating the question, asked herself, "Why am I still here?" Although she would never admit it to anyone, one reason why Balynda used to want her marriage to work was for appearances. She recalled his exact words when she confronted him less than a year into their marriage and he admitted to having an affair.

"Zeke, something is off. I don't feel like we're as connected as we used to be. Is there someone else?"

"Yes," he replied nonchalantly.

Taken aback, she yelled, "Get out. Go pack your bags and leave."

She never expected him to do what she asked. He never had before. So, when he was headed out the door, bags packed and all, she begged him to stay. Really begged him to stay, snotty nose and all. Admittedly, she played that one wrong. There she was with the upper hand, and she let him take back the position. "Never let 'em see you sweat." She had been trying to live up to that mantra ever since.

Now, she didn't care what other folks thought about her having a failed marriage. Heck, most marriages end in divorce nowadays anyway. She also professed to stay for the kids because she firmly believed that kids deserved to be raised by both parents. Her parents were still married after almost forty years. She cherished having her parents still together and often found herself bragging about their union. She simply wanted her children to have the same testimony. She saw how divorce seemed to complicate the lives of her grown friends and was glad that she did not have to add those concerns to her already hectic life. When she would go back to Columbia for visits, she did not have to concern herself with sharing her time between her parent's separate households. She could visit mom and dad all at once and she fully recognized that being able to do so was a privilege and honor. She wondered, however, if her concerns about her kids' bragging rights were less important than her mental health.

# ❧ Chapter Three

Balynda hurried into her cubicle with one minute to spare. She was always racing against the clock. Even if she was ahead of schedule when getting ready to go somewhere, for some reason, she started to slow down her pace and ultimately ended up being late. She couldn't figure that one out for the life of her.

"Good morning!" She chimed to Max, her office buddy across the way. She learned a long time ago to shake off her home problems at the office door. Not always an easy task, but it certainly made her days a little brighter. So, despite her tumultuous homelife, when Balynda went into work, she tried to put her best face forward and take work as it came.

"Good morning, Balynda!" Max responded with matched enthusiasm. Balynda reflected upon how wonderful it was to have such a great coworker. He looked like the office geek but was unexpectedly cool. They sat near each other for the past six years, and he had helped her get through many personal and professional challenges. Despite masking efforts, once someone taps into your heart, it is hard to hide life's pains from them. Max was one of those people for her. Once he realized the perpetual state of her marital discord, he stopped asking about her marriage.

"I am about to head down to the cafeteria and grab something to eat. You want anything?"

"Well, thank you, Max. That would be perfect. I have to meet with Attorney Lendon at nine. If you grab me a cup of coffee and a bagel, I can get ready for my meeting."

"All right," Max said. "I know how you like your coffee…decaf with cream and no sugar, right?"

"You got it," she replied.

"And a plain wheat bagel," they said simultaneously, and then broke into raucous laughter.

"We've been sitting across from each other for too long, huh?"

Max walked to her cubicle and leaned on the partition. "Yeah, I know your eating habits. That is how you stay so fit and trim. I admire that." While she beamed, he continued, "I, on the other hand, got to get my grub on."

"Quit playing. You look good, Max." She redirected her attention and perused the case file of Zakyia and Brian Smith Jr., the children from her most recent removal. Pressed for time, she hoped Max did not try to engage her in a full-blown conversation.

"I got you." Max turned toward the cafeteria.

"Oh, I know. I keep a mental tab."

Max shook his head. "You would do that."

"Thanks!" She chuckled. Her mood shifted as she considered the meeting with Attorney Lendon. Preparing emergency custody complaints was often wearisome. She had to convey everything about the family so the always-pressed-for-time agency attorney could condense it to a one-page complaint.

Rumor had it that Attorney Lendon, one of two Black female attorneys out of about twenty, was, quite frankly, evil. The agency was full of gossipmongers, so despite the cautionary notice, Balynda planned to meet her with an open, untainted mind. She was also aware that some busybodies kept tension rising by assuming that a sister in a position of power had to be a tyrant. Although she had met a few strong personalities along the way, she tried to give everyone the benefit of the doubt. To do otherwise was stereotyping and she had grown beyond that.

Balynda tried to immerse herself in the Smith matter, but images of Zeke popped into her mind. She wondered what type of relationship he had with Cindi. Cindi was the woman Balynda suspected was sleeping with Zeke. She had worked with him for the past eight months. Prior to Zeke's office holiday party, Balynda questioned his constant mentioning of Cindi and her frequent calls to his cell at inappropriate hours.

The night of the holiday party, Balynda and Zeke were actually enjoying one another's company until Cindi boldly sauntered into the ballroom. Her jet-black hair was neatly coifed in an updo, and her makeup was immaculate. She donned a tight, satin, emerald, green mermaid dress with a plunging neckline that would make any woman except J-Lo think twice. As soon as Cindi saw Zeke, she made a beeline directly to him and greeted him without even appearing to notice Balynda's presence.

"Uh, good evening, Cindi, don't you look fabulous?" Zeke said as he gently released himself from her full-frontal embrace. "This, this is my wife, Balynda."

Cindi attempted to act as if she had not even seen Balynda standing there previously in a deep conversation with Zeke. "Oh! Hello Balynda. Nice to meet you."

Balynda had no interest in pretending to be glad to meet Cindi, so she chose to instead respond with a soft nod of her head and an unconvincing smile. She certainly did not get a good vibe from Cindi nor was she able to ignore Zeke's nervousness with being in the presence of both ladies. Call it women's intuition, but she knew something was amiss. Perhaps it was the information her friend Tara had shared with her just days before the party that caused Balynda to be on high alert. Tara, Zeke's coworker whom Balynda adored, called to express her concern about Zeke's evident "friendship" with Cindi.

"Girl, they seem a little too close to me. I'm going to keep my eyes on them."

"What do you mean, Tara? Like, what are they doing together?"

"They are darn near inseparable! It seems like every time I see him, here she comes tagging along! And they are too giddy. Get on my nerves!"

Ever since then, Balynda began to pay closer attention to anything that pertained to, included, or had even a hint of Cindi. She did not want to let Zeke know Tara was watching them, so elected to play it cool and collect evidence. Based on what Tara had told her about Cindi, combined with her first impression, Balynda had made her case.

Max set the coffee and bagel on her desk. "Here you go, madam." Without looking up, she said, "Thank you so much, Sweetie. Your account balance is closing in on paid-in-full." She laughed, spinning in her chair to give Max her full attention.

"Yeah, okay. You really are keeping score, huh? Hey, I meant to ask you about that removal you had yesterday." He paused. "You okay?"

"Yes, it was a little crazy for a minute. I am so glad the police have to go with us now. Someone said that back in the day, we had to do this without any protection. Crazy!"

"Extremely. I was here then. If you were lucky, you might get a coworker to go with you," shaking his head, he continued, "but it wasn't as dangerous as it is now. When crack came on the scene, things really got ugly. Now, with the opioid epidemic, it would be suicide to go by yourself."

"You ain't never lied." She gathered her casework.

"All right, let me go do this complaint."

"Oh, that's right. Attorney Lendon is quite good. She is thorough and somewhat abrupt, but she gets the job done."

"Cool. I was a little concerned. I just want to get this thing done so we can be ready for the hearing this afternoon," she said, leaving her workspace.

"You'll be fine. You can handle her."

~ ~ ~ ~ ~

"Good morning!" Balynda sang as she entered the attorney Lendon's office. "I am Balynda Brown. Your nine o'clock," she announced right hand extended.

A stunning Black woman with an equally decorative office. She went beyond the typical family pictures and had two magnificent plants that brought life to the cozy space. Attorney Lendon was an obvious fan of animal prints as all her picture frames, contact paper and figurines revealed her favorite pattern. Even her Ohio Bar license was encased in a frame that showcased creativity and the skills of an accomplished interior decorator. Although she did not have an office with a window, the beautiful picture she had of an African landscape more than sufficed. The leopard slippers Attorney Lendon had tried to conceal under her desk sealed it for Balynda that this lady was more relatable than expected. With less enthusiasm, Attorney Lendon said, "Good morning. Nicole Lendon, nice to meet you." She stood, shook Balynda's hand then sat behind her cherry-stained oak desk. "You're here for the Smith matter, correct?"

"Yes. We removed the children from the home yesterday. This family is no stranger to the agency. The mother, Lena Young, has two older children who are in our permanent custody. Both have been adopted." She reviewed her notes. "The eldest child is in the legal custody of the maternal grandmother. Lena got herself together for a while, completed her case plan, and was permitted to raise the two we are here for today, Zakiya and Brian, Jr. She was doing great until she started dating the kids' father, Brian Smith, Sr."

Attorney Lendon did not utter a word as she rummaged through the case file and busied herself on the computer. Balynda paused for a response. She didn't want to interrupt the apparently essential task, so she tapped her pen on the file. With her gaze on the computer screen, Attorney Lendon said, "Yeah. Unfortunately, that is often the case. Let's take it from the top so I can confirm some basic information. Zakiya is a one-year-old female. Date of birth is October 24, 2014, correct?"

"Correct."

"Brian Jr. is a four-year-old male. Date of birth is July 18, 2011, correct?"

"Correct."

"A set of identical twins in permanent custody. That would be Zara and Zarita. Zehira is in the legal custody of the maternal grandmother, right?"

"Right."

"Huh, sounds like someone loves the letter Z."

"Apparently," Balynda chuckled.

Attorney Lendon took a deep breath and sat back, joining the chortle. "I like them, though." These names all have meaning. Zakiya is Swahili for pure. I was going to name my daughter that."

"I like that name and its meaning."

"Who adopted the twins?"

"They were adopted by a maternal aunt and her husband. Zehira has special needs. Coupled with her age, we considered it best for the maternal grandmother to maintain custody. She's great with the kids, but now also has custody of three of her son's children."

"In addition to Brian Jr. and Zakiya?"

"Yes, but they can't stay there long. That puts six children under her care. I am concerned it's too much for her. God bless her. She is doing all she can to keep her family together. The paternal grandparents have expressed interest in the children. We started background checks on them. Hopefully, that will work out."

Attorney Lendon shook her head. A somber mood with a hint of pity and tinge of disgust lingered in the air. "Thank God for grandparents. I admire these ladies. They raised their children and have to decide whether to raise their grandchildren or send them to foster care. Commendable." She exhaled.

"I see it every day. It's exactly why I do everything in my power to make sure these grandparents have everything they need for the children. Clothing vouchers, WIC, you name it. They don't need any extra burdens."

"No, none at all."

For the next thirty minutes, Balynda shared what she knew about the family. By the end of the meeting, she felt like she had found a new social companion. She admired Attorney Lendon's Ohio Bar membership and professionalism. Most importantly, she was impressed with how comfortable she felt in her presence. It was as if they had been friends for years.

"I'm a member of a social group. Sisters Inspiring Sisters or S.I.S. is a group of like-minded women who get together monthly.

We have attended plays, traveled, and even had a slumber party. Would you like to join us Saturday for dinner?"

"That sounds great! Where is dinner?"

"The new restaurant on Carnegie serves Cajun cuisine and has a jazz band. I think it's Rajun Cajun Kitchen or something like that. We want a maximum of twelve members and right now we have six.   We are looking for like-minded women who are professional yet love to get together and have a good time. We're meeting at 6:00 p.m."

"Count me in. Where do you stay? Maybe we can ride together."

"I was thinking the same thing. I stay in Cleveland Heights off Taylor Road."

"Cool. I stay in Shaker so you're not too far from me. I can pick you up."

"Sounds like a plan," Balynda said as she stood to her feet. The meeting had taken longer than her body desired as she had to shake off the numbness in her legs. The ladies exchanged numbers and made plans to meet Saturday at 5:15 p.m.  As Balynda left the legal department, she felt a sense of accomplishment. Not only had she made headway in the Smith case, but she may have made a new, much-needed friend.

# ◯ Chapter Four

Balynda and her coworker, Leslie, grabbed a quick bite for lunch before darting off to court. Leslie was one of her few White friends. They had only been friends for about two years, but it felt like a lifetime. In addition to having the same profession at Children and Family Services, they both were big superhero fans and shared a love of reading mysteries.

"So, did you find a good placement for the kids you removed Monday?" Leslie asked.

"Oh yes. They are with their maternal grandmother for now. I am trying to see if we have any other available relatives because she cannot keep them long-term. The paternal grandmother is actually looking like a possibility."

"You can't ask for much more than that." Leslie took an enormous bite of her sandwich filling her cheeks completely.

"Well, that was some kind of crazy, the boyfriend breaking out a gun and all!"

Balynda popped a few white grapes in her mouth. "Girl, I know. That has only happened to me one other time, but that was during training, and I was observing Amy. Miss Big-and-Bad was about to pee in her pants! Now that I think about it, that was a sign for me to get out while the getting was good. To top it all off, she is now my supervisor of all people! Talk about going from bad to worse!"

"Sad, isn't it? I never dreamt of being a caseworker as a child. I always wanted to be a dancer but all I kept hearing was 'How will you pay your bills?' or 'What are you going to do with that?' I mean, I get satisfaction from helping abused and neglected children, but the stress is too much."

"You know I know all too well. I feel you totally. I feel boxed in here. I understand the importance of what we do, but this is not my passion. I don't wake up every morning kicking my heels because I am coming in to work at Children and Family Services. This cannot be the end of my story. I can't see myself retiring from here twenty years from now. I won't make it!"

Leslie finished the last of her soda. "Well, have you had the chance to work on your health and fitness business lately?"

"Very little. It is so hard working with the agency full time and trying to hold things down at home. It takes all my energy to make it here on time every morning. I have been trying to narrow my focus. Since diabetes runs strong in my family, I was thinking about trying to become a certified diabetes educator. Now, that would be right up my alley. It would combine my love of teaching with my love for health and nutrition matters," she gleamed as she finished the last of her lunch.

"Now, that sounds like a plan. What all will that take?"

Balynda expelled a huge sigh. "I have the education requirements, but I don't have the required work experience. Basically, I need to become a health care professional working in diabetes self-management education for at least two years, which has proven hard to obtain due to my lack of experience."

"The old catch twenty-two." Leslie shook her head in disappointment. "Well, I have faith in you, Balynda. Keep at it despite the rejection letters. Some smart employer is bound to know a good candidate when they see one."

"If I can just get an interview, it is a wrap. I know my skills and knowledge of diabetes and nutrition will astound them. I just need a favor. Favor Lord!"

"Favor!"

As Balynda looked at her, she considered how grateful she was that Leslie had come into her life at this time. She hated to say it, but Leslie seemed to welcome her "dump sessions" without appearing to tire from the consistent complaints. She tried not to complain so much, but before she knew it, she was spilling her guts. *Leslie must be an angel sent from heaven to help me get it all off my shoulders.* Bellies full, they headed to juvenile court.

"By the way, have you heard any more about Cindi?" Leslie asked with a disdainful emphasis on "Cindi".

Balynda was not trying to give Zeke any more of her energy today. She was tired of dealing with the same old, same old. She was absolutely devastated when she found out he was still sleeping with his ex-girlfriend, Star, before they celebrated their first anniversary. She often felt that she asked for it, as she was the reason why they broke up in the first place. At the time, she knew he had a woman but figured that a girlfriend was replaceable. She would never date a married man but had no problem seeing a man with a girlfriend. The dating scene was too limited to rule out men with girlfriends. Star was in payback mode and could care less that *her* man had wed. Balynda learned that payback was a mother.

This thing with Cindi brought back all those painful memories. She had countless other clues and indications of him stepping out with other women, but without hardcore proof, he was not going to admit to anything. This time, however, she had reliable sources telling her that he was cheating. Couple that with women's intuition and old Zeke was cold-busted.

Balynda mustered a bit of strength. "Well, of course, he is telling me that it is all in my head. You know, the usual spiel. I don't know what to believe. I thought about calling her to find out the real deal. But you know what? I am tired. I don't have the energy to deal with this right now. I know he is working late more often than not. I just don't know. Frances told me to trust my gut and my gut is telling me they are an item."

"I understand. Pray about it and try, if possible, not to worry." She rubbed her friend's back. "What action you should take will come to you in time."

"Yeah, I know. To be honest, I am about all prayed out. I have been praying about my marriage since the first affair. Now, fourteen years later, I am still dealing with the same issue. I am trying to be a praying wife, but it is so hard! How do you pray for someone who hurts you over and over again? I am not quite sure how much more of this torment I am supposed to take." Balynda tilted her head back to fight off the tears as Leslie put an arm around her to comfort her.

"Weeping may endure for a night, but joy cometh in the morning." Then, they walked through the doors of juvenile court.

*Well, it has been a long night. Come on joy.*

~ ~ ~ ~ ~

As Balynda made her way to Judge O'Reilly's courtroom, she ran smack into Lena Young.

"Oops, excuse me, Lena. Hey, we need to sit and discuss your case. Ple —"

"Talk to my attorney. Anything you need to say to me, do it through him." She pointed toward Attorney Tom Stewart. Tom was a regular at juvenile court. He and Balynda had worked on multiple cases together.

"Okay, but he is just going to tell you to cooperate with me, so you might as well sit down with me now."

"Don't you tell me what I might as well do! You might as well talk to my attorney like I said because I have nothing to say to you." Lena turned and walked away in a huff. Balynda raised an eyebrow, smirked, and walked toward Brian Jr. and Zakiya's maternal grandmother, Ms. Young. She sat in the waiting area feeding her newborn grandson, who was recently placed in her custody. Zakiya climbed on and off the seat displaying her abundant energy. Despite Ms. Young's apparent lack of sleep and undeniably heavy load, she smiled when she saw Balynda approaching.

"Good afternoon, Ms. Young. You know you did not have to come for this emergency hearing, but I am glad you were able to make it. You never know what could go wrong."

"I know. You told me, but I don't want to miss anything. I wish I didn't have to bring the babies, but I had no choice. I took Brian Jr. to Head Start this morning to make things a little easier," she chuckled then propped the baby on her shoulder for burping.

"That's good. No need for him to be here. I am hoping their paternal grandmother shows up today since she is interested in keeping them long-term. I checked her out and things look good so far. What do you know about her and the rest of Brian Sr.'s family?"

"I have only seen or talked to her a few times. She has always been pleasant and very helpful with the kids. She knows her son has some issues and does not try to sugarcoat anything. That's what I like about her, she keeps it real. I told her 'I get it because my son is also out here making all these babies.' They just need to sit down somewhere."

"I hear you," she looked around for Mrs. Smith. "Well, hopefully, she shows up today to make herself known to the court. That will increase our chances of getting the kids placed with her."

Balynda sat back on the pew-like seat and tried to refrain from fidgeting. For her, waiting was the worst part of coming to court. As soon as she saw Attorney Roberts, she hopped up to greet him and let him know she was there. He was the prosecutor from the agency assigned to Judge O'Reilly's courtroom. They reviewed the complaint, and she gave him a complete update on the case. She told him how far she had progressed on investigating Mrs. Smith and explained why Ms. Young could not keep the kid's long term. As Balynda paced the floor waiting for her case to be called, an attractive brother walked in her direction. "Excuse me, Balynda Brown?"

"Yes."

"Hi, I am Dion Jiffries, the attorney for the father, Brian Smith, Sr. Nice to meet you." He extended his hand. Balynda was nearly mesmerized by Dion's flawless deep chocolate skin. His perfectly lined sideburns and mustache gave the appearance that he had just risen from the barber's chair.

"Nice to meet you, Mr. Jiffries. I assume the father is still in jail." Balynda muttered as she gathered her thoughts.

"Oh, yes. I'm afraid he is going to be there for a while. I don't think his parents are going to *bail* him out this time, in every sense of the word." Dion snickered enjoying his play on words.

"Yeah. He certainly has an extensive criminal record."

"It appears that he came from a good family. Not sure why he went astray, but it happens."

"No doubt. I don't think it's fair to blame the parents when a child goes wayward. Now, if you have multiple kids that are not doing the right thing, then parenting may be the problem."

"Right. No matter how perfect the home and parents, some kids are going to do wrong and make bad choices. I don't care what you do. That is not to say that they won't turn their lives around. It takes some folks a while to get it."

"Yep, I agree. Only so much a parent can do. Like I tell my kids, 'I can lead you to the water, but drinking is up to you.'"

She sat on the pew to rest her feet. "You must be new around here. I don't recall seeing you before."

"Just passed the bar exam and hung up my shingle. Not

wasting any time working for someone else because I know me. I am an entrepreneur at heart. Did a few internships and summer clerkships to get through, but now it is all about The Law Firm of Dion Jiffries."

"Well, congratulations. You have to give me some of your cards so I can help you get going."

"Definitely!" Dion searched his briefcase and handed her a dozen business cards.

The bailiff opened the courtroom doors and called for their case. She gathered her purse, briefcase, and the Smith case file then walked toward the courtroom with Dion following in ladies-first fashion. She saw Mrs. Smith bustling into the waiting area, smiled, and motioned for her to hurry. Judge O'Reilly was on the bench as they entered the courtroom. "Good afternoon, Your Honor," rang out as everyone went to their designated areas. The parties remained standing until told otherwise.

Sam, the bailiff, bellowed, "Case number JC904289, in the matter of Brian Smith, Jr. and Zakiya Smith for an emergency custody hearing, February 17, 2016."

Judge O'Reilly declared, "You may all be seated. Attorney Roberts, please present your case."

"Thank you, Your Honor. The mother, Lena Young, has been involved with the agency since 2001. She has three older children who have been removed from her custody: two adopted and one in the legal custody of the maternal grandmother. We removed Brian Jr. and Zakiya from their home on February 15, 2016. The basis of the removal was the mother's continued failure to abide by the requirements of her case plan and her lack of cooperation in our investigation of abuse and neglect regarding the children.

"On February 13, we received a referral stating that the children were visibly unkempt and hungry. In addition, Brian Jr. was observed with multiple unexplained bruises on his right arm. Unfortunately, we were notified after the children were back in the mother's care. The social worker, Mrs. Brown, was unable to access the home on the evening of the thirteenth and did not get a return call from the parents, Lena Young and Brian Smith, Sr. As such, we removed the children from the home Monday morning, at which time the deplorable conditions of the home were observed. I would like to call the caseworker, Balynda Brown, to the stand at this time."

Balynda rose from her seat and walked to the witness stand. She was sworn in by Sam before answering a series of questions from Attorney Roberts.

"What did you observe as you entered the home on February 15?"

"The home was filthy with dirty diapers, clothes, trash, and old food scattered everywhere.

The mother, Lena, was lying on the couch under the influence of some type of substance." Lena blurted from the defendant's table. "How do you know? You don't know what was going on w—"

*Bang! Bang! Bang!* Lena's words were caught in her throat as the judge slammed his gavel.

"Counsel, admonish your client to refrain from outbursts or she will be removed from my courtroom. Is that clear?"

"Yes, Your Honor." Attorney Stewart then turned to whisper in Lena's ear.

The judge turned to Balynda. "Please continue."

"The father, Brian Sr., was sitting on the couch next to the mother. When he realized what was going on, he pulled out a gun. He was apprehended by the police officers who accompanied me to the home."

Attorney Roberts questioned, "Once you were in safety, what observations did you make regarding the children?"

"Both children were dirty and very hungry. Brian Jr. had three bruises on his right arm. We took the children to the hospital to determine any other physical problems."

"You did not find nothing, did you? That's 'cause ain't nothing wrong with 'em. Y'all just-"

Tom tried to silence Lena's outburst, but he was losing the battle.

"Ma'am!" Judge O'Reilly slammed his gavel again. "Is there something you are not understanding? The next time you disrupt my court you are out of here! Are you clear on what I just said?"

Lena nodded and dropped her head.

The continued questioning revealed that the children were slightly underweight for their respective ages and although Brian and Zakiya were not born with drugs in their systems, there was enough concern to warrant continued involvement by the agency. Lena had a history of poor decision-making which was often at the expense of her children. Attorney Roberts introduced the photos of Brian Jr.'s black-and-blue arm into evidence.

"How did he get these bruises?"

Balynda sighed. "At four years old, Brian, Jr. knows that ratting on either parent would contribute to the unlikelihood of his returning home. He simply said that he fell down without any additional explanation." She looked at the photos and continued, "The paternal grandmother, Mrs. Smith is present today. She is interested in caring for the children. The agency's investigation of the Smith family is almost complete."

The judge looked at Attorney Stewart. "Cross-examination?"

"Yes, Your Honor. Mrs. Brown, are you a certified drug counselor?"

"No, I am not."

"Not a medical doctor or a nurse, correct?"

"Correct."

"So, you are not qualified to determine if the mother was under the influence of drugs?"

"I have seen enough peo—"

"That is a yes-or-no question, Mrs. Brown."

Although Tom was only doing his job, Balynda wanted to roll her eyes at him. Tom and Balynda already knew the judge was going to grant the agency's petition. They always did unless the evidence was clear to do otherwise. In Balynda's experience, most judges preferred to be safe rather than sorry and simply rolled with the agency's findings.

"I am qualified to determine, if a person," she paused for emphasis, "who has a history of abuse, is most likely under the influence of drugs if, at 9:00 a.m., they reek of alcohol, exhibit poor hygiene, and can't even—"

"May the Court take notice that Mrs. Brown refuses to give a responsive answer. I am going to move along. You don't have any proof that Brian Jr.'s bruises were inflicted by my client, do you?"

"No, I don't."

"No further questions, Your Honor." Tom sat.

The judge directed to Dion. "Counsel for the father?"

"Yes, Your Honor. Mrs. Brown, do you have any proof that the bruises were inflicted by Brian Sr.?"

"No."

"Although the mother has an extensive history with the agency, this is Mr. Smith's first involvement with the agency, isn't that true?"

"Yes, but as the mother's boyfriend and the father of two of her children, we asked him to comply with a safety plan. To date, he has failed to do so."

"No further questions."

Balynda was no attorney but knew Dion did not expect to gather more negatives about his client from that line of questioning.

"Let's see," the judge said, reviewing the court file. "We need guardian ad litem for the children."

The bailiff said, "I can see if anyone is hanging around out there."

"Okay. Go see who you can find. And fast."

Three minutes later, Sam returned with Attorney Bill Tully, the official juvenile court flirt.

*Here we go*, Balynda thought.

Bill asked every sister from the agency for a date. He had no qualms about letting anyone who asked—or didn't—know that he only dated Black women. He would probably fare better if he stopped giving his sales pitch to women who worked in the same building. Nobody wanted somebody who wanted any and everybody. The Court brought Bill up to speed on the case and assigned him as guardian ad litem—or GAL—for Brian, Jr., and Zakiya.

The judge remarked, "Based upon the evidence presented, it is clear that it is in the best interest and welfare of the children that temporary emergency custody be granted to Children and Family Services. Placement to remain with the maternal grandmother, Ms. Young until the agency determines that a more suitable relative placement exists. This hearing is adjourned."

The bailiff ordered, "All rise." Judge O'Reilly turned his gaze toward Dion. Looking over the edge of his thick bifocals, he stated, "I've never seen you around here before."

Dion darted to the bench and shared his private practice spiel. Balynda directed her attention to Mrs. Smith. She asked her about the progression of the background investigation and then spoke with Ms. Young about getting the services she needed to care for the children. She exited the courtroom and took a seat in the waiting area organizing her items and making notes. She was not up for talking to Lena anymore today. There was no convincing her that lack of cooperation was her doom.

"That went well." Balynda looked up to see Dion standing in front of her.

"Oh, yes. As anticipated. The only issue here is getting a good placement for these kids. I don't think Lena is ever going to get it together."

"Oh, ye of little faith! Sounds like someone is getting burnt out."

"Burnt out and pessimistic. I have seen this storyline so many times. She may turn it around, but I doubt it. Sorry to say."

He looked at his watch. "I may need to call you to discuss this case and get a better feel for how your agency works. May I have one of your cards?"

"Certainly." She retrieved her business card holder from her purse. "We can keep each other abreast of updates. Make this thing as simple as possible, you know?"

He placed her card inside his suit jacket. "For sure. Nice meeting you and I will talk to you soon."

"All right, same here."

After taking longer than usual to get organized, Balynda began walking to exit the courthouse. She wished she had a longer wait to avoid going back to the office. Before she reached the security officer's station, she heard a familiar "Hey Beautiful".

"Bill," she remarked earnestly seeking to hide her irritation. "What's up?"

"You are looking so divine today. I thought I would see if you're free for a cup of coffee or something. Anything, anything you want."

"Ha! Bill, you don't take 'no' for an answer, do you? You know I am married, and I have told you---."

"Yes, but are you happily married? And I am a gentleman. Of course, I take 'no' for an answer. But from you, I know your heart is really saying 'yes'.

"Goodbye Bill! I have to go back to the office anyway."

*Be careful what you wish for.* Balynda shook her head in bewilderment. *Sometimes, we are never satisfied.*

# Chapter Five

Balynda arrived home at about 6:30 p.m. with her energy depleted. When she returned to the office after court, she had to put out multiple fires given to her by Amy. Apparently, she was out of line for asking which matter took precedence over the others because Amy's response was wrought with anger. "What? What do you mean which one to do first? They all need to be done today!"

Balynda responded with a simple "Okay" and after Amy left her office, she hunkered down and got it all done. Getting it done, however, required that she work past her normal work hours and ignore the many phone calls she saw coming through her work phone. Something had to give so she figured the calls would have to wait.

As Balynda struggled through traffic on her way home, she called Frances to help her endure the ride. "Oh poo!" she exclaimed when France's voicemail message began to play. Instead, she turned on Praise 94.5 FM and joined in with Kirk Franklin's *Wanna Be Happy?* The song ministered directly to her soul and lifted her spirits. She entered their Tudor-style home, kicked off her shoes, hung her keys on the designated key rack then perused the mail. Zeke designed and established a mudroom right off the foyer after they moved in about nine years ago. The mudroom was perfect for her family as they all, adults included, had a bad habit of leaving their shoes laying a little bit of everywhere. While she loved the charm of their older home, she was yearning for a new home designed by Zeke as he had been promising her for years.

As Balynda looked in the local grocery store ad for coupons, May nearly knocked her over when she soared past her all decked out in green from her Girl Scouts activity. "Slow down, girl!" Although May's and Desmond's extra-curricular activities had her running endlessly, she would not have it any other way. An idle mind is the devil's workshop, and she refused to give the devil any tinker time with hers.

She headed upstairs to her bedroom to slip into her comfy clothes. She noticed that her clothes were starting to fit snuggly around her waist. Not big on scales, it was only when her clothes began to feel tight did Balynda even consider weighing herself. She struggled with accepting her weight in her youth and had to make a conscious effort not to be too critical of herself. She had grown being called "big hips" and "built". Even if some of the name-callers had no malicious intent, the labels only served to make Balynda excessively preoccupied with the numbers on the scale.

She hopped on the scale to find that she was almost at her maximum permissible weight, per her BMI, of 150 pounds. This was her typical winter weight fluctuation. She was not too pressed by the realization but vowed to start cutting back on Monday. She needed a few days to gear up for a period of no desserts and low carbs. At age thirty-eight with two kids, she was frequently complimented on her weight. However, she was also often told that her size must be inherited and that she simply cannot become obese. That position always bothered her because it dismissed the fact that people can lose weight with diet and exercise. She made a point of reminding such commentators that exercise is good for everybody, regardless of size and that it is wrong to assume that a person's size is automatically indicative of their health status.

After changing into her sweats, she headed downstairs to begin dinner. Tonight, she was preparing broiled salmon filets topped with her special béarnaise sauce over a bed of rice and a side of asparagus. She started the rice and grabbed the aluminum foil to lightly broil her asparagus. For the sauce, she replaced the egg yolks and butter with reduced-fat mayo and low- fat plain yogurt to create her healthy version of the delicious but fat-free laden sauce. She didn't mind cooking with a little butter, but an entire cup during her tip-the-scale season would not be wise. Her fingers were covered in salmon seasoning when the doorbell rang.

"Desmond! May! One of you guys answer the door, please."

Of course, Miss Nosey May made a mad dash for the door. Balynda peeked around the corner to make sure her baby was safe.

"Who is it, May?" No response. "May! Who is it?" Annoyed, she went to the sink, washed her hands, and headed to the door. As she approached the foyer, she heard a woman questioning

May.

"Well, do you know when he will be home?"

"No. Whenever he is done working."

"He is not at work. I can assure you of that. Well, did he—" Balynda pulled the door open further to see Cindi standing on her front porch.

"Thank you, May. You can get back to your homework," Balynda calmly stated, stifling her rising fury. May looked at Cindi then back at her mother. Without saying a word, her eyes seemed to say, "Don't hurt her too bad, Mama."

"May, go!" She pointed toward the kitchen. Not wanting to throw on her crazy-woman cape unnecessarily or hastily, she played Ms. Cordial instead. "Come on in, Cindi. It's freezing out there, and my heat is escaping."

"That will not be necessary. I just need to know where Zeke is." Her lips quivered.

"Please don't say that he is at work because he is not."

Balynda mentally prepared to toss her crazy-woman cape over her shoulders.

"Is there a work-related emergency that he needs to tend to? I assume you tried his cell phone."

"I have been blowing up his cell phone since five o'clock. And no, no work-related emergency." She rubbed her hands together for warmth or combat readiness. "Look, let's just keep it real. Zeke is my man, and I need to know where he is." Fastened cape, slipped on mask.

"Excuse me? You have some nerve coming to our house referring to my husband as your man! I mean, are you really that dumb? Do you think he calls you his woman? More like, his who…"

Cindi pointed her finger and moved within inches of Balynda's face. "Don't even think about it! Zeke and I are in love. We both know that I mean more to him than you have in years. Don't blame me if you don't know how to keep your man at home. When you find him, tell him I got something waiting on him if he's man enough to come home."

Speechless and stunned by each dart Cindi threw, Balynda slammed the door, leaned her back against it as her knees gave way, and slid to the floor. She wanted to reach her bedroom to avoid the children witnessing her break down, but the grief was just as heavy as her ragged breaths. The kids had already gathered to see why the door was slammed. They tried to get her up and tend to her hyperventilating, but she was too consumed in sorrow. Between tears and rapid breaths, she managed to tell them to call Frances.

When Frances arrived some twenty minutes later, the kids had managed to get Balynda into bed and breathing at a normal pace.

For some reason, every time she was troubled by Zeke, she found comfort in their bed. The fact that she gave no instructions to Desmond and May on where to take her revealed they knew it was her safe haven, as well. Once she entered her place of refuge, she gathered herself into a fetal position as May and Desmond placed the covers over her.  A river of tears continued to flow down her cheeks and saturated her pillow.  Without any hesitation, Frances finished making dinner and put the kids in bed. After caring for her best friend like she was on her death bed, Frances left around 10:00 p.m.

"Do you think Daddy is coming home tonight?" May questioned Desmond after Frances pulled out of the driveway.

"He better not. He is the last person Mama needs to see right now. I'm not having it!"

"Well, then I am going to lie in bed with Mama."

"I was thinking about doing the same thing. She needs us right now. Come on!"

The kids grabbed their pillows and climbed into bed with their mother. They both held her tight and didn't utter a word. Their presence awakened Balynda who had briefly drifted off to sleep. She wanted to hold on to them as well, but their grips were so fierce, she didn't dare try to break free.  *If the only good that comes out of this rotten marriage are my children, then I have enough.*

##  Chapter Six

The next morning, Balynda summoned all the strength she had for the sole purpose of preparing the kids for school. Just as promised the night before, Frances came by to take May to school. Desmond caught the bus, as usual, after first making sure his mother was feeling a little better.

"Oh shoot!", Balynda exclaimed after she remembered she needed to call Amy to let her know she was unable to make it to work.

"Hey Amy, good morning. I, um, am not able to come in today. I'm not feeling 100% and I need to take sick leave today."

"Really? This is such short notice. Have you gone to the doctor?

"No, I don't need to go to the doctor, not yet anyway. And I thought I had three days before I had to show…"

"Right, right," Amy interrupted. "I was just expressing concern. Ok, well, since you are not scheduled for court, we should be okay. I know you have quite a few follow-ups that need to be addressed but I guess one day won't be too bad. I hope you can make it in tomorrow."

"That is the goal. All right, have a good day."

Amy really had a knack for pushing Balynda's buttons. "She could at least pretend to care about my well-being, " Balynda pouted. On her way back to bed, Balynda passed a mirror. Her usual impeccably styled hair was now in disarray with the back matted to her head while the front and sides were pointed in every direction possible.   Her eyes were red and puffy with the corners revealing the unmistakable need for soap and water. Although Frances had selected one of Balynda's nicest pairs of pajamas for her to put on, she still looked like someone who had been crying uncontrollably all night and in need of much TLC.  Disgusted by her appearance and the state of her marriage, she quickly hopped back into the bed and buried herself under the covers. She began to question what she might have done wrong to cause her marriage to grow so sour. She considered herself to be a good catch. She was smart, well educated, attractive, a great cook, a great housekeeper, and a good mother. She had never cheated on Zeke, and she always gave him whatever he desired to the best of her ability. She never refused him sexually and always wanted to make sure there was nothing another woman could give him that she could not. He often complained about her moodiness and their lack of shared interests, though. Was that enough to cause him to be unfaithful. Shouldn't her good qualities outweigh the bad ones?

Balynda had made efforts to get involved in things he enjoyed doing. She tried to like outdoor activities such as hiking, mountain biking, and fly fishing. She had come a long way with her moodiness. She truly believed much of that was hormonal and beyond her control, and that he should be understanding regarding her dislike for her job and the city. The phone rang interrupting Balynda's sulking. She didn't bother checking the caller ID before answering.

"Hello?"

"How are you feeling, girl?" Frances asked, her voice laced with concern.

"Lying here trying to figure out what I did wrong. I mean, he really is a good man. He is a great provider and good-looking. I know many women would love to have him. So, how did I let this happen? Why can't I keep him satisfied?" She burst into tears. "What is wrong with me!"

"What?" Frances shrieked. "Oh, Lord. That man has you brainwashed. Girl, the only thing wrong with you is that you have a sorry husband. From what I can see, you have done everything a good wife is supposed to do. Honey, a man like that will never be satisfied for long. You could swing butt naked from a chandelier, and he would still not be completely satisfied. Balynda, it is not you; it is him."

Balynda's sobs slowed to a trickle as she clung to every word Frances said. "You have to realize that a cheating man is going to cheat, despite what you do to try to keep him from cheating. Sure, you are supposed to do what a good mate is supposed to do. But if you have truly given your all and he still wanders, girl, let it go. You do not control someone's decision to be faithful. That was Zeke's choice alone." Frances paused. When the silence went unanswered, she called out to her distraught friend.

"Balynda? Balynda! Are you still there?"

"I'm here." She wiped away tears. Everything Frances said hit a chord with her, but it did not take away the pain. She expelled an exasperating series of sighs.

"Okay. I need to come back over there. What time does May get out of school?

"Four o'clock."

"All right. I already told her to look for my car if she does not see yours. I will pick her up and stay for a while. I hate to ask, but have you heard from Zeke?"

"If he has called, I don't know anything about it. I guess he spent the night with… Cindi." The mention of her name caused Balynda to stammer as a lump formed in her throat.

"Oh, well. I know you're hurting, but girl, the hell with him! That is the attitude you need to have. The hell with him!" The passion in her voice matched that of an actress auditioning for a full-length, drama-suspense motion picture.

"You are so right. Pray for me. My heart is so heavy it hurts."

"I know. Time will heal all. Try to rest and put your mind on Jesus."

~ ~ ~ ~ ~

A few hours later, Balynda was awakened by a hovering presence. Leaning over her like a traditional Japanese bow of respect, Desmond stared into her face. She opened her eyes.

"Hi."

"Hi, Mom. How are you feeling?"

"A little better, thank you."

"Mom…"

"Yes?"

"Your breath really stinks. And you look a mess. You should get up and do something with yourself."

She cracked a smile. "Thank you, Desmond, I think. Perhaps it is time I do just that, huh?"

"Uh, yeah. You may start to feel better."

*Out of the mouths of babes.* She questioned Desmond about his day and then rolled out of bed.

She spent several extra minutes brushing and flossing her

teeth followed by rinsing. She started to comb her hair, but after a few unsuccessful tugs, she realized nothing was going to help that hair but a good shampooing. When she stepped out of the shower, May ran into the bathroom. "Daddy's on the phone!" she exclaimed, handing her the cell phone. She shooed May out of the bathroom.

"Hello?" she answered softly.

"Hey. Listen, baby. I am so sorry. I don't know what's wrong with me. I—I need for you to forgive me. Let me come and talk to you."

Balynda had not thought about forgiving Zeke. Her focus was on getting over the pain.

"Zeke, I am tired of going through this with you. If I let you sweet talk me into coming back, I will be in this position again. You obviously want to be single, so do you."

"No, Balynda. I don't want to go through life without you. We just need counseling or something. I will come by tonight, and we can talk about it, okay?"

"I have to think about that. I need more time."

"All right, baby. You call me if you and the kids need anything. I know Frances is over there with you guys." He paused. "I love you, baby. You know that, right?"

"Love me? No, Zeke, I don't know that. You don't put

people you love through this much pain. If this is how love feels, please don't hate me."

She hung up the phone without waiting for his goodbye. "He has a lot of nerve." She agonized over Zeke's infidelity. She was coming out of the slump he'd thrown her into, but his phone call disrupted that progress and sent her back into the fire. She could not believe he expected her to forgive him. She knew he had not changed and was operating from guilt since he got busted. She rationalized that forgiveness today would result in another heart-wrenching situation in a year or two, per his usual modus operandi. She reflected on his mention of counseling, a new tactic for Zeke. She contemplated scheduling a session in the hopes that it was all they needed to get on track.

Other than Frances, she had not called on anyone because she knew that they couldn't help. The only person that could help her out of this mess she had not called on but decided now was the time. She walked back into her master suite and knelt in front of the bed with her hands in prayer to ask God for direction. "Help me, Jesus," was all she said before her eyes welled with tears flowing freely down her cheeks. After taking two deep calming breaths, she continued.

"Lord, you know the situation. You know my heart and You know I have done all that I know to do. I am at a loss, so I am turning to You. Please lead me and guide me. Help me make the right decisions. Heal my heart, Lord. If You don't do it, it won't get done. Please, Jesus." She sobbed as she climbed into bed with wet hair, a damp bathrobe, and drying skin. She slept peacefully, despite vague memories of Frances, Desmond, and May checking on her. Frances apparently thought it best to spend the night, as she entered Balynda's room with breakfast at 6:30 a.m. Although she refused all previous requests to eat, she gobbled down the scrambled eggs, turkey bacon, and toast quickly—barely pausing to breathe. Needing a second day to pull herself together, she then called in sick again to Amy. After helping Frances get the kids off to school, she sat back, relaxed, and watched her favorite daytime shows.

"Thank You, Jesus," she said as she thought about how much better she felt. Yesterday she was agonizing about how she was going to move on from Zeke because she would miss the good memories too much. They had shared so many good times together, how could she disregard all that and end their marriage? God showed her that if she decided to leave Zeke, that choice had nothing to do with the good memories they have shared. Their memories would still be there for her to cherish. Beyond that, she could create new and better memories. She knew the Lord would bless her latter days greater than her beginning.

She had cried her last tear of heartache over Zeke and declared he had officially lost his control over her heart. She surmised that she gave him control years ago, and in those years, he did not take good care of her heart. Even if she didn't rush out to end the marriage in divorce, she affirmed her intention to take back her heart.

Deena C. Miller Wingard

# ❧ Chapter Seven

After tossing her belongings on her desk Monday morning and briefly chatting with Max, Balynda checked her voicemail messages.

"Twenty-two messages!" she expressed aloud, "Gadzooks!" She sat in her chair and grabbed a pen and paper to take notes. She had multiple calls from attorneys, mothers, fathers, grandmothers, drug treatment facilities, parenting programs, coworkers…, and so on. You name it; there was a message. Moving on to the thirteenth message, Balynda was a little surprised at what followed.

"Hello, Balynda. This is Attorney Jiffries calling about the case concerning Brian Jr. and Zakiya Smith. Please give me a call when you get a minute. You can reach me by calling 216-555-0354." She briefly admired his DJ-like voice and then continued listening to more messages. The fourteenth one also came from a familiar voice.

"Hello, Balynda. This is Dion again, the attorney for Brian Smith Sr. Uh, you know I am new at this juvenile law thing. Give a brother a call back. I have a few questions for you. My number is 216-555-0354."

"Give a sister a chance, Dion." She hoped he did not think she was going to do his work for him, as it would be in his best interest to talk to some fellow attorneys. After listening to the remaining messages, she decided to call Dion first since he left two messages. Plus, his voice was quite soothing.

"Hello, this is Balynda Brown. How are you doing?"

"Much better now that I am hearing from you. I thought you social workers were supposed to be more punctual in returning calls," he chuckled.

"I don't know where you heard that. Unless you state your matter is urgent, it may take a minute. Do you know that I am responsible for sixty-five open cases?"

"Oh, I know you guys have way too much work. I am just messing with you. So, how are you doing, besides having too many cases?"

"Uh, much better." She released an audible sigh. "I needed to take a couple of days off." Balynda figured that was enough information for Dion.

"Well, glad to hear you are doing better. Anything I can do to help?"

*Why is he acting like we are old friends?* "Uh, no, I will be okay. Thanks for asking. So, what can I do for you?"

"I wanted to talk about my client's case plan. I was thinking maybe we could discuss it over lunch or something. Then you can bring me up to speed on juvenile court. We can also get to know one another better. I can see already that I need to make some friends in this line of business!" *Very interesting*, Balynda thought. *Is he hitting on me or just sincerely wanting to talk business? Only one way to find out…*

"Dion, I typically don't go out to lunch with other men since I am a married woman. Now, I do make an exception for strictly business."

"Dang girl, you don't hold back, do you?"

"I am too busy for that," she quipped.

"Hey, I hear you, might as well keep it real. Well, to begin, I had no clue you were married. What is a beautiful married woman like yourself doing walking around without a wedding ring?"

"It no longer fits me properly. It's constantly sliding around my finger and coming off all the time, so I chose to put it up before I lost it. Unfortunately, it came up missing after a house party a couple of years ago."

"Okay, now. No, having lunch with you would not be strictly business, as I was drawn to you as soon as I met you. I would really love to get to know you better. So, tell me, when can you spare an hour or so to tell me more about yourself?"

Balynda pondered for a moment, stunned at Dion's interest

in her. When she first met him, she did not even think of him in that manner. Sure, he was a nice-looking brother, but she thought nothing more of him. The idea of having a relationship beyond business never occurred to her… until now.

"I am flattered, Dion, but I have a lot going on right now. Plus, I try to do the right thing and I don't think this would fit in that category."

"Ahhh, just trying to get to know you, Balynda. Being intimate with you is not my motive. I just want a little of your time. That is all I am seeking—your time."

"Well, let me finish returning these calls, and I will get back to you. We do need to catch up on our case anyway. I will try to get back to you today. If not, first thing tomorrow morning."

"You have my cell phone number. You know you don't have to wait until tomorrow to call me. If you get a minute tonight, I would love to hear from you."

"Okay. Talk to you soon."

Balynda sat back in her chair and stared at her blank computer monitor. Countless men had tried to talk to her during her marriage. She would always shrug them off or clearly express her lack of interest. This time, however, she wondered if it was timing or chemistry, but Dion had undeniably piqued her interest.

~ ~ ~ ~ ~

After Balynda picked up May from aftercare, they made their usual Friday stop at Redbox to grab some movies for the evening. May picked out a Disney movie that she did not have in her collection but had seen a zillion times before. Balynda didn't even bother calling Desmond to see what movie he wanted to watch. He had recently grown uninterested in family time, choosing instead to occupy himself with his Play Station IV in the solitude of his bedroom.

When Balynda and May walked through the side door of the house, the first thing Balynda noticed was the aroma of Zeke's infamous seafood gumbo. "Hmmm…. Very interesting," she said setting the movies on the kitchen bar stool and looking in the direction of the chef taking control of her kitchen.

Zeke roared from the kitchen, "Well, good evening, ladies! I am almost finished making my favorite ladies, my favorite dish!" Balynda could not resist the smile that formed on her face as Zeke's favorite dish, chicken parmesan stuffed peppers, was also one of her favorites. Zeke was undoubtedly trying to warm her heart.

Poor May did not know how to react. It was obvious she was excited to see her father, but it was also apparent that she was still angry with him for causing her mother so much pain. She did not know whether she should embrace or ignore him. Solving her dilemma, Zeke took hold of May and gave her a huge hug. May grinned profusely and resolved to relish in her father's company. Balynda mumbled, "Good evening. No need to order pizza tonight, I see."

"Nope, not this Friday, Love." Zeke moved closer to Balynda. "I tried to surprise you with a little something, something." Zeke stroked her hands and then pulled her toward him. With his right arm embracing her, he tenderly located her ear amongst her long, deep brown hair. He leaned in close, and whispered, "I need you. Please forgive me. I promise you. I will do better."

Balynda's heart melted as her high school sweetheart wooed her. She did not want her marriage to end. The thought of being a single mother concerned her. Life was hard enough raising the kids with two parents. She did not want to be the family at school events with the absent father. Perhaps Grandma was right after all when she said that a piece of a man is better than no man at all. "We can talk about it later, Zeke." Balynda released herself from his hold. She looked at him with welcoming eyes, and without saying a word, allowed him back in.

~ ~ ~ ~ ~

Balynda awoke Saturday morning to sizzling pork bacon and cinnamon rolls. She smiled as she thought of how hard Zeke was trying to get back in her good graces. As she relieved her bladder, she talked to herself about her prodigal husband.

"If he could only stay this sweet and attentive. Maybe he has really changed this time. I guess whatever he and Cindi had was not all that." She flushed and washed her hands. "He is here with me and wants to keep our marriage alive. If he is really done with her, I think we can make this work."

Balynda donned her robe and proceeded downstairs to quiz Zeke.

"Turkey bacon too, right?"

"Girl, I have only been gone a week or so. You know I know what you like."

"That pork is really smelling good," Balynda smiled.

"Lip-smacking! So, how did you sleep?"

"Really good. I am starting to get used to sleeping alone."

"Well, get unused to it because I am coming back in the bed tonight."

"Oh really? What will Cindi think of that?"

Zeke visibly took a large inhale and slowly released the air silently. He then rubbed his forehead and cleared his throat. His here-we-go expression made her sigh.

"I knew this was coming," he set the grease-laden fork down on the counter and looked at her. "But you held off longer than I thought. Cindi is history. Despite what she told you, we were not kicking it like that. We hooked up one time, which in her eyes, made me her man. She is a little off if you didn't notice. Now, I have to figure out what to do about her working for me."

"I guess you should have considered that before you had an affair with your subordinate. You stuck yourself with a mess that is affecting your livelihood. Not smart, Zeke!" She broke off a piece of bacon and popped it in her mouth. "So, are you telling me that you and Cindi are through with this little fling or whatever it was?"

"It has been over. I told you she was bugging out. She threatened to tell you if I cut her off and that is just what she did. She meant nothing to me. I was," he paused, "just being dumb is all."

"Real dumb. Now you got this crazy woman coming to our house creating chaos for the whole family. Do you realize how much this has stressed the children?"

"I know, babe, and I am going to correct my wrongs. I can't move forward if I keep dwelling on my past mistakes. I need you to forgive me, so I can make it right."

Frustrated with more empty promises, she turned and left the room. She spoke over her shoulder and then proposed, "The question is how *long* will it be right?"

~ ~ ~ ~ ~

Balynda rummaged around in her closet hoping to find the ideal outfit for the S.I.S. outing that evening. She landed on a winter white pants suit and matching three-inch ankle boots as if purchased as a set. She accented the ensemble with a long silk scarf adorned with her favorite soothing colors of chocolate, caramel, and burnt orange. Zeke had brought the scarf back for Balynda after a business trip to Dubai. Of Zeke's many faults, gift-giving was not one of them. He would often lavish Balynda with gifts or give her his credit card for no apparent reason at all, stating, "Go buy yourself something nice."

"Oh yes!" She gave herself a final glance in the floor-length mirror before heading downstairs.

May saw her mother heading for the coat closet. "Can I come, too, Mom?"

"Not tonight, baby. S.I.S. outing tonight." She reached for her camel-brown cashmere coat and tossed it over her shoulders. "Is it supposed to snow some more tonight?" Balynda asked over her shoulder said to whoever was listening.

Zeke sat in his chair with his feet propped up reading the newspaper and watching a Bruce Lee movie. "Not tonight, but you know how that goes. They say no snow, but we get a foot." He looked over at his wife and did a blatant double take. "Uh, where are you ladies going again?"

"The Rajun Cajun Kitchen on Carnegie." She adjusted her scarf. "There's some chili in the fridge. You can make some cornbread to go with it if you want."

"Dear, I am not the babysitter. I know how to find something for my kids to eat, thank you. I think we'll go out for dinner as well."

"Okay, do you. I was just trying to help you out." She leaned over to give May, who refused to leave her side, a big hug and kiss. "Mommy should be home in time to tuck you in tonight, okay?"

"All right." May bowed her head and pouted.

"When it is my turn to plan a S.I.S. outing, I will make sure it includes the daughters of the members. We can do something special like get our nails done or go to a ritzy restaurant. How does that sound?"

"What is a ritzy restaurant?"

Zeke answered, "One in which daddy passes out after he sees the credit card bill."

Balynda darted her eyes gallingly at Zeke.

"Yeah, right." She opted to not take a hat then headed for the door and yelled up the stairs.

"Bye, Desmond!" She stepped up two stairs, looked at her watch, and then redirected toward the door.

Desmond flew down the stairs practically swinging from the handrail. "See ya, Mom!"

"Slow down, fella!" She relished the chance to give him a hug and a kiss.

Zeke got up from his chair and walked to Balynda. "Have a good time, dear. Try not to have my ear burning too much tonight, okay?"

"Oh, you can forget it!" she chuckled. "You are definitely going to be a topic of discussion."

Zeke shook his head. "Are you driving? I thought you were riding with that new attorney friend of yours."

"Something came up, so she is going to catch up with us a little after six. I hope she makes it because I think she would fit in well. Well, time to go!" She reached out to embrace Zeke. His six-foot-three frame felt so good that for a fleeting moment, she pondered staying home to engage in a stress-relieving, make-up session. Something about him made her forgive him physically before her mind agreed to do so. She shook off the temporary lapse in judgment and whispered gratitude for having plans for the evening. She was in no hurry to do something that she would beat herself up over in the morning. She struggled to maintain the upper hand and it was too soon for all of that.

~ ~ ~ ~ ~

When Balynda arrived at the restaurant, she constituted the fifth member of S.I.S to make an appearance for the evening. The four members already present each had their guests sitting next to them at a table set for twelve.

"So nice to finally put faces to all of your names," said Balynda as she was introduced to all the guests. Each of the first six members had to obtain an application from the ladies they hoped to add to the membership. The six reviewed the applications then all affirmatively voted on the candidates. Balynda already knew three of the first six and, after one outing, knew she had made two more life-long friends.

"Girl, you look good!" Frances complimented.

"Thank ya, honey. You are looking awfully nice yourself! I love that blouse."

Balynda assumed Frances wanted to say something like, "How did you go from looking like a heap of mess to that in a matter of days?" Her canned reply would be "Jesus." Because only God could keep her from looking like what she had been through. To take Frances out of her misery, she continued, "I had a pretty rough week, as you know." She pulled out the chair next to Frances and sat. Frances leaned back in the sturdy yet body-conforming chair in anticipation of the impending bash fest.

Lisa, one of Balynda's pre-S.I.S. friends, kicked off the

questioning. "What was so rough about it?" She looked back and forth between Balynda and Frances as she realized she was not in the loop. Balynda sighed. "Well, Zeke's infidelity was confirmed… again. His lil' mistress came by the house to tell me to my face." The ladies gasped. Their astonishment shifted to anger and disappointment.

"He has some freakin' nerve!" Lisa banged her glass of Merlot on the table. "How dare he put you through this crap again. Girl, no ma'am, uh-uh, not again. I am steaming!" After wiping the Merlot off her hands, she began to pat her feet and rocked in the chair. In a calming tone, Balynda, said, "I know it. So, you can only imagine my pain. It happened over a week ago, and I am just now getting back to some sense of normalcy."

"So, what are you going to do? Are you two going to try to work it out or what?" Kim, who was fairly new to the group, asked.

Although Balynda considered her a friend, she regretted offering such intimate information to so many in such a setting. She stammered, "I, I don't know. I have so much to consider." I should not have brought this up. My apologies."

Lisa said, "Girl, please! That's what friends are for. If you're not okay, I'm not okay.

"When you hurt, I hurt," Lisa stated.

Lisa's sincerity and saddened gaze pierced Balynda's tear-filled eyes.

"Dang it! I said I was done crying over that dude, and I certainly had not planned to cry over him tonight. We are supposed to be having a good time. Let's talk about something else."

"That's cool. But let me just say that if my husband even considered cheating on me, he would get cut!" Tamara, Frances' guest, chimed.

Frances gave Tamara a high five. "Girl, I know! I am sorry but somebody is getting sliced."

The ladies roared with laughter.

"Y'all stop playing! I ain't doing time for nobody. I'd be locked up, and he would be out having fun with some of everybody."

"I'm not kidding. We don't play that where I'm from. I bet he would think twice next time," Tamara added.

Attorney Nicole Lendon looked a little uncertain of her entrance but walked to the table to join the group after making eye contact with Balynda's familiar face. Standing to embrace her, she beamed, "Hi, Nicole! So glad you could join us." Directing Nicole to the seat next to her, she continued. "Everyone, this is my guest, Nicole. She is an attorney at my job."

"Good evening, everyone. Please excuse my late arrival. I ran into some unexpected delays," Nicole stated.

"We understand. We're glad you were able to join us. It's a pleasure to meet you," Frances exclaimed.

As Nicole took her seat, Geneva and her guest, Yolanda, arrived to complete the party. The ladies had a fabulous time dining, laughing, sipping wine, and engaging in deep, meaningful conversation. Balynda gave no more energy to Zeke until her departure as she neared home. The pangs of her marriage tried to seep into the elation that the time with her friends gave her spirit, but she held those thoughts captive and dismissed them from her mind. "Not tonight," she intoned as she exited her car. "Not tonight."

# ⟡ Chapter Eight

Zeke nudged Balynda, "Time to get up, sleepyhead."

She stretched. "For what? The kids can get their own breakfast."

"No, silly. It's time to get ready for church. We missed the seven-thirty service but we can catch the ten-thirty. Let's go!"

"Are you serious? When was the last time we went to church as a family?"

"My point exactly. We are doing a new thing! The Brown family will be going to church together every Sunday from here on out."

She looked at Zeke in disbelief as she rubbed her heavy eyes. She recalled the last time Zeke called for a renewed family commitment to attend church. It was right after he got busted having an ongoing relationship with Star. That church commitment lasted all of one month, once he figured she wasn't going anywhere. She wondered if he really believed God was so stupid to think that his church attendance was sincere. What made him think that God did not notice he only attended church when he messed up or needed something? When things got better or no respite came in his desired timeframe, Zeke disappeared from the church house until the next crisis struck.

She moaned, "All right, all right. What time is it anyway? Are the kids up?"

"It's almost eight-thirty and of course not. I figured I'd start with the slowest."

"Whatever!" She threw her pillow at him.

He dodged the anticipated reaction with a Keanu-Reeves-in-The-Matrix lean as he headed out the bedroom door. He chuckled as he strolled toward May's room to disturb her rest. The family spent the next hour searching for decent church attire, gobbling breakfast, and scrambling out the door. Balynda was surprised that the children did not render any objections to going to church. She surmised that they were happy that Mommy and Daddy seemed to have weathered another storm and that the family was still intact. She had to admit that going to church as a family felt good to her as well and found herself envisioning this as the new norm. She reminded herself not to get too excited based on Zeke's predictable yet torrid past.

~ ~ ~ ~ ~

The Browns arrived at church in time for the pre-sermon song. After an electrifying praise-and-worship experience, Pastor Lovett preached a powerful sermon. The message was Balynda's favorite part of service, and Pastor Lovett never disappointed. Pastor Lovett bellowed, "The ax is at the root of the tree! Galatians 5:19-

21 tells us about the works of the flesh." He continued with an old-school Baptist hum. "Sexual immorality, impurity, sensuality, idolatry, sorcery, enmity, strife, jealousy, fits of anger, rivalries, dissensions, divisions, envy, drunkenness, orgies, and things like these. God said that it is time out for continuing in sin! He sent me to warn you that those who do these things will not inherit the kingdom of God! Turn to your neighbor and say, 'The ax is at the root of the tree!'"

Satisfied that the message was directed at her wayward husband, a smug Balynda turned to him with full force and said, "The ax is at the root of the tree!"

Zeke's shame shadowed his flawless skin. Try as he might, his eyes betrayed the guilt he fought to hide. His countenance did not lessen Balynda's elation that the pastor stepped on his size-eleven shoes.

"God called us to bear the fruit of the Spirit. If you are not yielding fruit, I have come to tell you that you are at risk of being cut down! But here is the good thing about God," Pastor Lovett shimmied as if stirring up the gift, "even when you mess up, God has a way for you to escape damnation through His Son, Jesus. Jesus is the Way, the Truth, and the Life! No man comes through the Father except through Him! You need only repent and return to God with your whole heart. Not just in pretense, as in Jeremiah 3:10, but truthfully acknowledge your guilt and your faithlessness."

Balynda side-eyed Zeke. Her harsh gaze was sent to remind him of his repeated unfaithfulness to God and her. *Ooh, I am so glad we came today.* She was beyond pleased that God was letting Zeke have it.

"And God, in His faithfulness to us even when we are unfaithful," continued Pastor Lovett, "will seek our return to the fold. In Jeremiah 3:14, God says return, O' faithless children, and I will heal your faithlessness. Return! And I will bless you! Who wouldn't serve such a mighty and merciful God? I'm so glad God is not like man! Folks will not let you forget the mistakes of your past, but God, in His grace and mercy, looks at the heart."

Balynda squirmed in her seat as she realized the finger was now pointing at her. While she was questioning Zeke's motives and enjoying his chastisement, God reminded her that her faithfulness also had room for improvement. She looked at Zeke expecting to again catch his gaze, but this time in judgment toward her, yet Zeke continued to look straight ahead and focus on the preaching before him. Balynda faded away in thought as the sermon began to explode in celebration. She wondered what God meant. Although she had resolved to try and work out her marriage, she had not fully sought God's counsel. The idea of truly forgiving Zeke's infidelity again just didn't feel right to her. The message, however, was clear. She needed to stop judging him and perhaps even let it go. But how?

## ❧ Chapter Nine

Spring was finally starting to settle in, even though it had officially started a month earlier. Springtime in Cleveland seemed brief, as winter sometimes refused to let go until May, then the early summer heat popped in from nowhere and took over before time. It was near the end of April and Balynda was sitting at work rummaging through case file after case file.

"I am so utterly sick of this," she said aloud, partly to herself and partly to Max. He simply looked over in her direction and continued working without rendering a comment. "There has to be a better way to make a living," she exclaimed, slamming down her pen, and sitting back in her chair. She then began to gaze at some of May's and Desmond's artwork and slid into a daydream. She reanalyzed every career-related decision she had made that brought her to her current position. Before coming to Children and Family Services she worked for a non-profit agency that simply did not pay her enough money to cover her portion of the expenses. Even though Zeke would tell her not to worry about the money, she always wanted to have her own and not be dependent on him. Amy's voice grew louder as she determined to get her employee's attention.

"Balynda, Balynda!"

Startled, she straightened up in her seat and looked at her

supervisor.

"Hi, Amy. Sorry, I was in deep thought."

"So, I see. Have you completed the report for the Andrews family that I asked you about yesterday? I told you I need it ASAP."

"Uh, I am still working on it." She pulled the file from under three others. She had almost completed the report yesterday when she realized she needed to make a few more phone calls. She could have submitted it as it was, but she took pride in her work and refused to submit anything half done. She awaited return calls from the Guardian ad Litem and father. "I was waiting to—"

"Balynda, I'm not interested in your excuses. I have the director asking me about this report. You have until close of business today to send it to me." Amy stomped down the hall without a further word.

Flabbergasted, Balynda flopped in her chair. Amy was known to be a workplace bully but that was the first time Balynda experienced it to that degree. As she tried to gather her composure and allow her blood pressure to simmer down, Max came to her desk to make sure she was okay.

"That was just uncalled for," he said with a loud whisper. "She didn't even give you the opportunity to explain or give a status. How rude!"

Balynda took a deep breath as she searched for the phone number for the GAL. She tried to overcome her feelings of humiliation and anger while she reviewed the Andrews report saved on her computer. "Yeah," she muttered. "Prime example as to why I despise this place. She wouldn't even hear me out. No concern for quality here, just quantity."

Max tiptoed back to his cubicle because he dared not give Amy a reason to direct her aggression toward him. As Balynda picked up the phone in a final attempt to reach the assigned GAL, she found consolation in her determination to resume her job search.

~ ~ ~ ~ ~

After cooking a healthy dinner of only beans and veggies, Balynda sat at her laptop and perused jobs for diabetes educators. Unless she obtained a degree in health care, she would likely not become a certified educator. She learned that she could opt for a diabetes care-related certificate that might assist in her career transition. May ran her fingers along the desk. "What are you working on, Mom?"

"Oh, I am trying to decide if I want to get a certificate in insulin therapy or continuous glucose management. This training will help me take care of your great aunt and maybe even help me get a new job."

"I hope you do get a new job because I am tired of hearing

you complain about your boss, court, and taking those kids."

Balynda looked at May, contemplated her reaction then shook her head. May was right. Her job was consuming, and she felt the stress growing. She knew that stress was not of God, but the bombardment of life issues made it difficult to stay optimistic. Her career was a major source of stress, which was why she was working to make a change. Her action gave her some peace and based on May's comment, she had to work on complaining less.

"Yeah, you are right, baby." She reached for May's hand. "I am working on it and I'm making progress with getting a certificate. It's a great place to start."

"That's good, Mom. The one about insulin sounds good. Aunt Ida has to take her insulin two times a day, and she always gives Wanda a hard time."

"It's settled then." She was excited as she registered for the twenty-hour course. She closed her laptop with a sense of finality and went into the den. She cozied up with Zeke. He had been the model husband the past few months and she savored his presence at home. While she was grateful that he was seemingly changing for the better, she was unable to accept that he was a new man. She secretly waited for the old Zeke to reappear and believed it was only a matter of time.

# ❧ Chapter Ten

As Balynda listened to her voice messages at work the next morning, she found herself feeling more relaxed as she listened to another message from Dion.

"I'm starting to feel silly only being able to leave messages on your work phone. I promise to respect all that you have going on if you give me your cell number. At any rate, uh, I'm just trying to get a case update, you know, on the Smith family. Please return my call. You have my number."

She had made a point to only call Dion when she truly had case updates or questions and avoided his requests to sit down for lunch or simply meet face to face. Quite honestly, she did not trust her own curiosity about Dion and had enough sense to stay clear from temptation. The custody hearing for the Smith family had been rescheduled a couple of times to give Lena more time to work on her case plan. Dion was also handling Brian Sr.'s criminal charges and beating that was their priority. Brian Sr. was perfectly fine with his mother keeping the children in her care, even though she had repeatedly expressed an inability to do so long-term.

The agency had decided to pursue temporary custody of Zakiya and Brian, Jr. despite Lena's progress. Lena's past was simply too checkered to overlook. Balynda made it a point to really help the parents get it together because she realized the cards were often stacked against them once Children and Family Services entered their lives. The problem was, however, the failure to be tough on the parents would sometimes backfire and unfortunately result in the death or serious injury of a child. Balynda did her best to help the parents or guardians, at the end of the day, she had to do what was best for the children. She had not lost a child yet, and for that she was grateful.

Remembering that Leslie was off work caring for her sick mother, Balynda figured today was a good day to meet Dion for lunch. She reasoned that they could talk about the upcoming custody hearing. After all, he would not be the first male colleague she had lunch with, so perhaps, it wouldn't be harmful. In the back of her mind, she could not ignore the thought that Zeke had a full-blown affair with Cindi. Surely her going to lunch with Dion paled in comparison.

"Good morning, Dion. It's Balynda. How are you?"

"Hey, hey, Beautiful," he stammered, surprised, and delighted to receive her call. "How are you?"

"I am well, thank you. Are you free for lunch today?"

"What!" He danced happily in his seat. "You are going to let me take you to lunch? Heck yeah, girl! I am at your beck and call. Shall I pick you up at your office?"

"No, no. I can meet you at Shorty's at noon. Does that work for you?"

"Absolutely! Absolutely. I am looking forward to it. Girl, you made my day."

She chuckled, "You are silly, Dion. See you soon."

As she hung up the phone, a sense of euphoria caused a big smile to spread across her face. She updated her case files with a little more zeal and glee as she anxiously awaited her lunch date.

~ ~ ~ ~ ~

Shorty's was a small, quaint mom-and-pop restaurant a few feet away from the south entrance to the juvenile court. All the courthouse regulars could be spotted there on any given day enjoying the American and Irish cuisines. The cozy dining room was always packed with patrons seeking to find at least a corner of a table available so they could sit down and speedily dine on some freshly cooked and delicious food.

Dion was already inside and seated when Balynda arrived. He stood up to greet her and helped her take a seat. She thought about how Zeke recently resumed this practice with her but had neglected to do so for many years before. She found such gentlemanly acts of chivalry to be ever so telling about how a man feels about the woman in his presence. She had no doubt that all men knew about these acts of chivalry, and the choice to not do so spoke volumes.

The small talk focused on juvenile law and their cases in common. She was amused by how fervently he devoured the double-sized corned beef sandwich he ordered. Opting to have a light lunch, she selected the garden salad with a scoop of tuna salad. She covered the entire salad with a mixture of ranch and Italian dressings and dug right in. Balynda found herself laughing a lot more than she had in quite a while which caused time to quickly escape them both.

"Oh, shoot," she exclaimed when she realized she had been gone from the office for over an hour, "I better hurry up and get back before my pesky supervisor starts looking for me. That woman is working my last nerve."

"See, that's exactly why I work for myself. Other than judges, I control my schedule. I can't do it."

"Oh, I don't blame you. I would love to be totally self-employed. I am working on some things."

"Well, let me ask you this," Dion said as he scooted his chair closer to Balynda. "Why is your husband having you working in a job that you don't like? I mean, as the provider, I'm not going to have my wife miserable in her career. I am all for women doing what they love and helping with the family dynasty, but I refuse to have her waking up every day going to a job that only disturbs her peace.

It's my job to make sure everyone in the household is good and functioning to the best of their ability. If you were my wife, I would encourage you to quit your job and pursue what brings you happiness. I would take care of the rest."

She deeply gazed at him as she thought about how good everything, he said sounded to her. Zeke made good money but never once gave her the option of quitting her job to "find herself." She snapped out of the trance when she reasoned that Dion was just running a line on her.

"I am sure you say that to all the girls," she responded with a chuckle.

"Naw Beautiful, I mean every word of what I just said. If you take the time to get to know me better, you will learn that for yourself," Dion declared as he stared directly into Balynda's eyes. "I'm not trying to brag, but I don't have to run game on women to get with them. There are lots of beautiful, single women here in Cleveland I can seek to be with. But you, you are who I'm trying to build something with. I know you are married and all, but something tells me that you are far from being *happily* married. And that—that is just a shame because I find you to be an amazing woman. I just want to get to know you better. That's all. Can you allow me to do that?"

Balynda squirmed as she readjusted herself in her chair and reached for her purse. Dion had already taken care of the bill, and she realized that for multiple reasons, it was time for her to head out.

"That sounds doable," she finally said as Dion also stood up to exit the restaurant.

"Nice, nice," Dion beamed with a smile that could melt even the coldest of hearts. She smiled in return as they exchanged a few more pleasantries, then departed ways. She continued smiling, even after he was no longer in sight, as she thought about the wonderful time they had together and his request to get to know one another better. She had no desire to be more than friends with Dion; thus, saw nothing wrong with longing to see him again.

# ❧ Chapter Eleven

Balynda found herself living more and more for the weekends as work grew increasingly difficult to endure. Although she found it rewarding to save children from abusive, dependent, and neglectful situations, it was the process and procedures established by management that drained her physically and mentally. She knew in her heart and soul that she gave 100 percent and beyond in her work. Therefore, it shook her to her core when her sincere efforts were only met with skepticism and hostility. As a natural leader herself, she found the management style of those placed over her to be unacceptable and downright ineffective.

She had learned over the years that if she put all her hopes and desires into her job, she would be left feeling disappointed and weary. As such, the start of her diabetes certificate program was exactly what she needed to put her eggs in more than one basket. Even if the certificate did not lead to a job, she was enjoying the process and found her studies to be a great distraction from her troubles.

To put some of her online training to practical use, she made it a point to care for her Aunt Ida, who was trying to rebound from uncontrolled diabetes. Aunt Ida had seemingly been managing her own health care until she was found in her bathroom unresponsive.

She had suffered an episode of diabetic ketoacidosis and would have died had her daughter, Wanda, not found her in time. Ever since then, Aunt Ida lived with Wanda and had been doing better. Wanda welcomed the opportunity for respite from caring for her mother with open arms. Her daughter and only child, Wanita, and her two young children also lived with her. Wanita was studying to obtain her bachelor's degree in mathematics from Cleveland State University while working part-time at a local restaurant. Wanita could not offer Wanda much help in caring for Aunt Ida and, in fact, needed her to help out with the twins. Balynda's visits to Wanda's home made her feel ashamed that she had not been there to help her family earlier. The visits allowed her to see how full her cousin's hands were and how much help Wanda needed but never asked for.

Wanda was sandwiched between caring for her mother, daughter, and grandsons. Once Balynda got a handle on giving Aunt Ida her oral medications and insulin, she told Wanda to take care of her needs and not worry about the household. Since then, Wanda would come back hours later looking refreshed after a day of pampering or running errands.

One of Balynda's biggest challenges was figuring out how to work the blood glucose meter to test Aunt Ida's blood sugar level. Aunt Ida absolutely hated pricking her finger and gave Balynda a struggle whenever it was time for the test. She was amazed at how her aunt, once a devout, no-nonsense, Christian lady, turned into this fibbing, non-compliant patient. She learned not to trust a word Aunt

Ida said about her care because nine times out of ten, Aunt Ida said whatever was needed to avoid any pricks, injections, or discomfort whatsoever.

Knowing that diabetes is often hereditary, Balynda vowed to do whatever she could to prevent being diagnosed with this serious disease. She appreciated the opportunity to help her family and to see how passionate she truly was about diabetes education as a career change. She really desired to smoothly transition from one career path to the next. If she could just hang on at Children and Family Services, that would work nicely.

Balynda found herself becoming busier as she sought to juggle her time between her studies, Aunt Ida, her family, and her job. She didn't count her increased time spent with Dion into the equation although she surely should have. They were now meeting for lunch whenever Leslie was unavailable, which Balynda helped facilitate whenever it was doable without requiring a lie. She considered her time with him "me time" because it was all about her. They would laugh and enjoy each other's company the entire time. She found being with Dion to be good for her soul and if they were not physical, she rationalized, *No harm no foul.*

After almost two months of having regular lunch dates with Dion, Balynda felt it was time to run her new friend past Frances. She had mentioned his name to her before in passing but strictly on a professional level. She began to feel as if she was keeping something from her best friend, and that did not sit well with her. Balynda and Frances were chatting one evening as they always did during her drive home from work.

"So, you remember Dion, that attorney that I have mentioned to you a couple of times, the one I have a couple of cases with?"

"Um, I think so. What about him?"

"Well girl, we have been going to lunch together, like, on a regular basis. I really enjoy—"

"I knew it!" Frances interrupted. "I felt you were up to something, but I didn't want to say anything. I wondered why you haven't been griping about Zeke."

"Well, we are just friends," Balynda couldn't control her desire to giggle or harness her smile. "All we do is go to lunch and have great conversations. He is really a nice dude. And like you said, he keeps me from dwelling on Zeke and his shenanigans."

"What is Zeke up to now?" Frances asked as her tone changed from excitement to anger.

"Oh, he has not done anything new. In fact, he has been doing quite well, from what I know. But you know it is just a matter of time."

"Don't I know it!" Frances agreed wholeheartedly. "Honestly, I don't know how you have put up with Zeke for this long, but that isn't my business. I just know that you seemed to be very upbeat and giddy lately, in light of all that is going on in your marriage. I did not know it was this Dion, but I did wonder if there was someone in the picture. Well, honey, it is not my place to judge you or tell you to go for it. All I can say is, Zeke has been asking for it for years. So, just be careful whatever you do. Love triangles do not usually end well."

"Girl, ain't no love triangle! I have no intention to take it further than it is now. But he has already grown on me, and quite frankly, I do not plan to stop spending time with him. He helps brighten my days."

"Well, honey, do you! I'm not mad at you. Perhaps I will meet this Dion one day."

"Yes, perhaps," Balynda stated as she pulled into her driveway. Even though she kept telling herself, and now Frances, that she and Dion were just lunch buddies, she really desired to see more of Dion. Although he had not asked yet, she would be open to expanding beyond their lunch dates. She felt as if there was so much more she wanted to see and do with Dion.

As she ended her conversation with Frances, grabbed her purse, and headed into the house through the garage door, she reflected on how he was such a gentleman. Never once had he tried to touch her inappropriately or push the relationship beyond her level of comfort. Sure, he should not have his sights on a married woman, nor should she be entertaining thoughts of him, but oh, how even the thought of him made her happy!

# ◌ Chapter Twelve

It was an in-office afternoon for Balynda as she had no court appointments or clients to visit. As usual, she used such days to catch up on her paperwork and make and return phone calls. Such days were also slower paced causing her to create the routine of getting an afternoon coffee and sweet treat as a pick-me-up to get through the day. If she felt up to it and had the time, she would often see if Leslie or Nicole was free to join her. Knowing that her supervisor was anal, Balynda made sure to go during her designated break to avoid any issues with Amy.

Balynda and Leslie had just arrived back at Balynda's cubicle after returning from a coffee break. They were in the midst of a good conversation, so they continued to chat while enjoying their freshly brewed beverages.

"I'm not trying to have any more kids, so I am not concerned about the Zika virus," Balynda proclaimed. "I am not letting no mosquito stop me from traveling."

"Well, I do want another baby, so I am staying away from any of those places on the list. I'm going to listen to the CDC," Leslie added.

"You know your husband cannot travel to those places either, Leslie, because he could pass it to you," Max chimed in.

"What! We are staying in Cleveland until this pandemic is over," Leslie declared. Balynda chuckled, "It's not a pandemic. It's an epidemic. It's only a pandemic when it spreads to several continents and has infected millions of people. I think the most recent pandemic was the swine flu."

As the trio chatted, Nicole turned the corner and joined the conversation. She was on a phone call when they went to the cafeteria, so she decided to stop by Balynda's desk and catch the tail end of her break.

"There is always something going on in the world we could be worried about," Nicole stated. "I just say, 'Put on some bug spray and keep it moving!' Sorry I missed you two."

"No problem," Balynda reassured Nicole. "We got—…"

Out of nowhere, Amy appeared putting a halt to the conversation. Her face was as red as a cherry, and her eyes raged with anger.

"Balynda! You cannot possibly still be on break. I sent you two emails requiring your response today, and I have not received anything from you. Have you—…"

Balynda interrupted, "Your emails said I have until the close of business. It is not the close of business. And yes, I actually have two more minutes left in my break."

She felt her blood boiling through her body, and her hands and her voice began to tremble in fury. She knew that when provoked she could have a bad temper and she felt it bubbling. She looked to see the reaction of her friends and noticed that they had all scattered like terrified children.

"Well, just get back to work," Amy ordered. "You have too many assignments due to be engaged in all this chitter-chatter."

"I said my break is not over."

Amy had already started back up the hall and continued her agitated walk as if she could no longer hear Balynda responding. Balynda paced in her cubicle for a few seconds to collect herself and lower her blood pressure. She realized that her anger caused her breathing to become labored, so she worked to gain control of it while she could. She sat down in a huff but could not do anything but replay what just transpired.

Within a few minutes, Max tip-toed over to her desk and whispered, "Hey, don't let her get to you. She was so out of line, but don't let her get the best of you." Balynda could only nod her head in agreement as she tried to log onto her computer to resume working. At that moment, her phone rang; it was Leslie.

"Oh, my goodness!" Leslie exclaimed in a low tone, "Just who does she think she is? You don't have to take that from her!"

Before Balynda could respond to Leslie, Nicole's extension

was displayed on the screen.

"Hold on Leslie."

"Hi, Nicole."

"Girl, what is wrong with your supervisor? She doesn't have the right to talk to you like that. I mean, she seriously violated your right to not be harassed and intimidated, especially in front of others! You should not let that slide."

"Really? What can I do?"

"File a grievance or something. I would talk to the union if I were you. You have a right to work in a hostile-free environment. She can't treat you like that."

Balynda had never utilized the union before but had always heard great things about the work they did. Knowing that she had an advocate to help her get some sort of relief from Amy or even an acknowledgment of being mistreated made her feel calmer and more at ease. After quickly ending her conversations with Nicole and Leslie, she called the in-house local union president and made an appointment to meet with him Monday morning. She resolved that being productive at work the rest of the afternoon was shot, as she was no longer able to concentrate.

Frank Mann, the union president, told her to take sick leave for the rest of the day and send Amy an email advising her of the same. She packed her work bag, gave Max a lackluster goodbye, and headed for the door. She didn't like to use the word "hate," nor did she believe it was right to have such an emotion, but when it came to Amy, Balynda felt it was the closest related sentiment.

~ ~ ~ ~ ~

Balynda took her time going home since she felt the need to keep moving. She wondered if she was experiencing nervous anxiety as she aimlessly walked around Beachwood Mall. She found the walking to be therapeutic as it gave her the chance to relax and calm down before going home to care for Zeke and the kids. As she thought about Zeke, she decided to give him a call in a continued effort to get her negative feelings off her chest. The call went unanswered and straight to voicemail. She was not surprised as it was approaching 4:00 p.m. which was still early for Zeke's typical workday hours. She opted not to leave a message and continued to peruse the mall. She did make a point to grab her favorite fragrance, Chanel, and some knick-knacks for the house.

She figured she should at least try to make it home before May made it in from gymnastics practice. She was so grateful that she and a few other mothers on the team had created a carpool arrangement to make life easier for themselves. She was only responsible for driving the girls home once a week and found her newly acquired free time priceless. She grabbed some dinner on her way home as she had no desire or even the stamina to cook dinner that evening. Picking up dinner made her again think of Zeke. She called him and yet again—no answer. This time, Balynda's mind began to wander as she wondered if he was with Cindi. *Or what if,* she thought, *he decided to get back with Star? Perhaps he has met someone entirely new? Oh, how I just want to tell him about my day!*

She kept thinking about him and wondering where he was during dinner, during her interactions with the kids, and as she lay alone in their marital bed preparing to end the day. True, she had retired to her room early, but he had been gone since 7:00 a.m., and it was now approaching 9:00 p.m. Her thoughts tormented her as she agonized about what Zeke was doing, and then vacillated to her stressful day at work. She replayed the embarrassment she felt when Amy chastised her in front of her colleagues. She felt belittled and disrespected. Her anguish began to mesh into a twine of mistreatment that she visualized enlarging into a large yarn-like ball with her entangled inside.

"I deserve better," she said aloud, addressing both issues that sought to overcome her mind. She began to think about God and her confidence that He would see her through any situation. Her next thought was of Dion. It was as if her Godly thoughts were under attack by her desire to fix the situation herself. *Hmm, I could call Dion. He always knows how to cheer me up.* Balynda contemplated for a moment, rose in her bed, grabbed her phone, and sent Dion a text message.

Balynda: Hey there.

Dion: Hey, you. What's up?

Balynda: I'm lying in bed alone. I had a crappy day at work.

Dion: Oh, really? Can you chat?

She called him and shared everything that happened at work.

He listened, never once interrupting until he was sure there was a question before him or a desire to hear his response. They talked for what seemed like minutes but was over an hour. Zeke called twice while she had Dion on the phone, but she declined the calls. She refused to interrupt the brightest part of her day to hear Zeke's excuses.

"Let's do lunch tomorrow, somewhere special," Balynda suggested.

"Oh, yeah? What do you have in mind?"

"Mmmm, let's go to the lake. We could eat lunch out there, but those seagulls are vicious," she laughed. "So, we can walk around the lake then grab lunch later."

"I like that, I like that. I have court tomorrow afternoon, so I will pick you up at noon. Sleep tight and don't worry about anything. Tomorrow is a new day."

"Thank you, Dion. I appreciate you. See you tomorrow."

The garage door opened. Calm surrounded her as she turned off the light on the nightstand. She did not want to confront Zeke tonight, or at all. To her own surprise, her concern had been minimized and she didn't care that he was just getting home. She rolled over and drifted into a peaceful sleep.

# ᐁ Chapter Thirteen

Zeke was already up and about when Balynda's alarm sounded. Before her feet could even touch the floor, Zeke began to explain his whereabouts.

"I already know you think I was up to no good, but I wasn't. Paul and I were out trying to wine and dine some new potential clients at Adega. We had such a good time that the evening escaped us. The good news is, they have decided to go with our company. This contract is huge!"

Zeke had a smile on his face from ear to ear. He looked so convincing that Balynda almost bought his story.

"Yeah, okay Zeke," she muttered, "tell me anything. Just like all the hundreds of other times you "worked late," she said, gesturing air quotes. "I'm just not buying it anymore, so you do you, and I'll do me."

"What does that mean?" Zeke asked as his forehead creased in wonderment.

"Just exactly what I said. I don't have the energy or even the ability to care anymore."

"Well, I don't know what you are saying to me, but I have to get to the office, so we can finish this conversation later," he said as he walked over to Balynda and kissed her on her cheek. "Have a blessed day, Balynda."

"Uh-huh."

She had grown numb to Zeke and his antics. She truly felt as if she no longer cared what he did.

"Stick a fork in me," she said to herself as she made her way to the bathroom to get ready for work. She briefly wondered if it was Cindi again this time, but then she swiftly dismissed that thought replacing it with images of Dion.

She decided she wanted to look extra cute today in anticipation of her lunch date. Since jeans were permitted at work on Fridays, she took extra efforts to doll up her outfit along with her favorite pair of jeans. She layered her Pyer Moss tank top with a matching white tunic. She adorned herself with her finest custom jewelry and paired everything with her matching purse and shoes also by Pyer Moss. She truly admired Kerby Jean-Raymond's designs but was first drawn to his social activism for the oppressed in America and his strong political conscience. She figured if she was going to wear designer clothes, she preferred to wear clothes helping a cause dear to her.

Balynda rushed the kids out the door to get them to school as she fumbled to make sure she did not forget anything.

May, who never missed a beat, acknowledged, "Mom, you look great." She eyed her mother up and down, "What's the special occasion?"

"Can't a mama look good for the sake of looking good?"

Of course, you can, but you usually don't, especially not on a Friday."

"Yeah, Mom. You got a lot of extra stuff going on," Desmond chimed in.

"Y'all be quiet. May, get in the car," she chuckled. "You two make me think that I need to do better." She kissed Desmond goodbye and then escorted May to the car. She checked her makeup in the rear-view mirror and then smiled, satisfied with her work. Two can play this game.

~ ~ ~ ~ ~

Balynda wanted to bury her head in her work all morning to avoid a repeat encounter with Amy. Nicole, Leslie, and Max all reached out to Balynda to make sure she was okay. Each one emphasized how out of line Amy was for berating her in front of everyone.

Balynda watched the clock all morning. She could not wait to get some fresh air and time with Dion. She left her desk around 11:45 a.m. for one last pamper check and to ensure she was downstairs on time for Dion's arrival.

Dion pulled up on time in his 2016 Jeep Sahara. Like always, he got out to help her get seated.

"My, my, my... You look amazing!"

She looked away from his gaze. "Thank you."

"I was thinking about getting corned beef sandwiches after our walk, but I would hate for you to get that white dirty." He shook his head. "Girl, I feel like I need to take you somewhere special!"

"Just being with you makes me feel special." She batted her eyes, sighed, and then did a mental girl-get-it-together check. "You are so refreshing."

He looked into her eyes and gently grabbed her hand. She did not refuse his touch. They chatted and laughed all the way to a perfect parking spot near Lake Erie. After Dion parked, he walked around to Balynda and reached for her hand to assist her out of the Jeep. She pulled back her hand.

"Remember, I am married." She reminded him.

Puzzled, Dion obliged and led the way to the lake's shore. They enjoyed each other's company and relished the beautiful, natural scenery. The temperature was in the mid-80s, but a blissful breeze emanated from the lake, making the weather bearable. Balynda's soft curls danced in the air as she resisted the urge to move into Dion's intimate space instead of walking a professional two feet apart. Holding his hand in the Jeep felt natural but public displays of affection concerned her. Her apprehension, despite her decision to elevate this relationship to the next level, spoke volumes. She wasn't sure if it was due to her concern about what others may say or because she knew adultery was a sin. The dilemma felt like an angel on her left shoulder and a devil on the right.

Despite her conflicting emotions, she agreed to have dinner at his place the following week. She tried to convince herself that it was innocent, but she knew that was a lie. With passionate chemistry oozing from every pore, "dinner" would likely entail more than steak and lobster. Back at the office, he helped her out of the jeep. "You'll be okay. You can face whatever is waiting for you in there." He held her hand a few extra seconds and gave it a soft squeeze.

"Thanks."

Careful not to attract unwanted attention, they said their corporate goodbyes with a handshake and wave. Balynda recited the Serenity Prayer as she trudged into the agency.

$$\sim \sim \sim \sim \sim$$

Wanda texted Balynda late in the afternoon.

Wanda: Hey, B. Can you come over tonight?

Balynda: Got some work to do. What's up?

Wanda: I need you to watch Aunt Ida. I have to study for finals.

Balynda: I'll be there.

Of course, she'd have to tend to the boys too, but she did not mind. This last-minute request offered her a legitimate reason to avoid finishing the conversation with Zeke. She was done with his excuses and lies. She didn't know what she wanted to do with her marriage, but she had reached her breaking point. Balynda spent the first thirty minutes organizing Aunt Ida's empty pillbox. She noticed several new prescriptions, so she called Wanda to confirm.

"Yeah, her iron has been low, so the doctor put her on B12 tablets and a daily multivitamin."

"Gotcha."

As Balynda sorted through twelve different medications and prepared her aunt for an insulin injection, she felt sorry for her. She sympathized with how difficult it must be to have your health, and thus, quality of life dependent on medication. As if clairvoyant, Aunt Ida said, "My life is in God's hands. Sure, this medication helps, but when God says it is time for me to go, it is time for me to go. This here old body belongs to Him."

"That's right, Aunt Ida." Her sorrow turned to admiration as she considered the endurance, she must have to keep pushing day by day.

"So, baby," Aunt Ida said without looking at her, "God has shown me some things about you. I don't know what you are doing, but God said, 'Stop.' Whatever it is you are doing or thinking about doing, don't do it."

Bewildered, Balynda looked at her aunt waiting to see if she had more. Aunt Ida took the medication and resumed watching *Golden Girls*.

"Hmmm," she tapped her chin, "Ok, I receive that."

Focused on the television, Aunt Ida replied, "All right then."

While part of her looked forward to alone time with Dion, her spirit was unsettled. Her flesh wanted more than a platonic friendship. She didn't want another friend. She wanted to show Zeke that he was not the only one who could "have fun." But even more than revenge, she wanted to feel love, respect, and genuine care. She wanted to ask her aunt, "Do I not have the right to be loved? Why do I have to stay in a marriage of disrespect, dissatisfaction, and disgust? What does God have to say about that?" Instead, she rose to prepare dinner. Too embarrassed to tell her aunt about her feelings for another man, she took her questions to God.

# ❧ Chapter Fourteen

Balynda gave Zeke the cold shoulder all weekend. He knew she did not believe his story, yet he did not relent in trying to convince her otherwise. She spent Saturday tending to the house and the kids. She also found herself spending a great deal of the day chatting and catching up with Frances and Lisa. After speaking to them both separately for hours, they decided to do a three-way call. The ladies had such a great time on the phone that they made plans to meet for lunch the following week. Balynda had not been able to make the last two S.I.S outings and she really missed time with her girlfriends. The laughs she shared with Frances and Lisa were just what she needed to get her mind off work, Zeke, and what to do with Dion.

Sunday morning, Zeke brought Balynda breakfast in bed. He set a cup of brewed coffee, fresh fruit, and French toast sprinkled with powdered sugar on a wicker tray. He knew that she liked her maple syrup warmed and was careful to do just that. She sat up in bed. "Hey, this is really sweet of you. What is the special occasion?"

"No special occasion. I just want to show you that I really am trying to make our marriage work. I can tell you don't believe that I was out working late the other night, but I can prove—"

"No, Zeke. I am just, so done with all this. I can't even

process or even handle any more excuses or lies. I have just simply had enough."

"What does that mean, Balynda? That you have had enough? What are you saying?"

"Zeke, I don't even know. I just know that I cannot take any more excuses, lies, fabrications, whatever! I'm just done with that. My mind, my brain, cannot hold anymore. I, I don't know what that means for our marriage. I guess I am still trying to figure it all out."

"Well, let's do counseling. We haven't tried that before," Zeke pled.

"I would simply tell a counselor the same thing. I don't have the capacity to be hurt by you again."

Zeke stepped away from the bed and looked at her with sadness in his eyes. After what seemed like minutes, he said, "Well, time to get ready for church. I'll get the kids in motion. Let's go."

Although she really did not feel like getting up and pressing her way through church, she knew she needed to go. She had been seeking the Lord about what to do regarding her marriage and realized that the least she could do was get up and go fellowship with others. Her soul was heavy, and she found herself looking forward to participating in praise and worship.

~ ~ ~ ~ ~

The family was able to pull into the church parking lot, park, and be seated inside the sanctuary all before the 10:30 a.m. service began. Although they had been going more often since Zeke's declaration, they certainly had not been attending every week. Today was the first time they arrived before service started, and Balynda realized that was because she made an effort to do so.

She felt God's presence throughout the service. During the opening prayer, she went up to the altar and even got down on her knees before the Lord and the congregation. While praying, she was reminded that in God's presence there is fullness of joy. She realized that was what she had been lacking. She had allowed the cares of this world to steal her joy. Every song sung during the service touched her heart, and she found herself weeping incessantly. The gatekeepers brought her tissues at least three times; she wished she had brought her own handkerchief. When Pastor Lovett rose to preach, the Spirit was so high that he tried to start the sermon twice but stopped so the Spirit could freely move.

"Glory!" he bellowed. "I know that this sermon is for somebody today. But I don't have no better sense than to let the Lord have his way!"

The shouting music took off again and entire rows of folks got up and broke out in praise dances. Balynda and Zeke were on their feet stomping and clapping their hands.

"All right, all right. In the book of 1 Corinthians 6:19,"

Pastor Lovett finally interrupted. "I am reading from the NIV. And it reads: 'Do you not know that your bodies are temples of the Holy Spirit, who is in you, whom you have received from God? You are not your own.' Lord use me, your messenger, to bring your word to your people. In the blessed name of your son, Jesus, Amen."

While Balynda was eager to hear the Word, she was certainly enjoying the praise break. She took her seat but still felt the Spirit of God moving within her.

"In our Scripture text," continued Pastor Lovett, "Paul has written to the church in Corinth. Over the course of all of chapter six, we see that the believers then were dealing with some of the same things believers are dealing with today. I don't care how much we advance in technology some things are just going to stay the same. It may be done a little differently, a different process, but in the end, the act is still the same. Sin is still sin! Oh, I know y'all don't want to hear about sin this afternoon. Somebody is thinking 'Why did he slow down the service for a sermon on sin?'"

The congregation chuckled with laughter. Balynda was actually thinking that very thing. She closed her Bible and listened intently to the messenger before her.

"But God is speaking to somebody today. Somebody needs to be reminded that this fleshly covering does not belong to us. Once you have accepted Christ as your Lord and Savior, you belong to God. I don't know about you, but for me, that is good news! That means I don't have to worry about fighting my battles because my battles belong to God. I don't have to worry about tomorrow because my God promised to never leave me nor forsake me. I belong to God!

"What you have to understand, is that you have been bought with a price. You are no longer your own. So, since you belong to God, you can't just do anything to or with God's body. I just come to tell you today do not be deceived.

"Look at verses nine and ten. '...Neither fornicators, nor idolaters, nor adulterers, nor effeminate, nor abusers of themselves with mankind, nor thieves, nor the greedy, nor drunkards, nor slanderers, nor swindlers will inherit the kingdom of God.' This is not as per Pastor Lovett: this is the Word of God!"

Balynda reached for her Bible again to look at verses nine and ten. She contemplated her upcoming plans with Dion. While she knew adultery is a sin, she just wanted to see it again for herself.

"Just because you can do something, doesn't mean you should," bellowed the preacher. "The Word says not everything is beneficial for the body. You can't live any way you want and still be considered righteous. Christians, by the very definition, are to be united with Christ. You can't be united with Christ, have God's spirit within, and defile God's temple. You have been bought with a price. Jesus gave his life for you on Calvary. Therefore, you must honor God with your body.

"You honor God with your body by living according to the Word of God, by eating right and exercising, by taking care of your health, and staying away from substances that only serve to cause you harm. Do you all know that gluttony is a sin? Some of y'all act like you don't know how to do things in moderation, but I come to tell you that you can do all things through Christ who strengthens you! You can get your health back. You can resist the temptations of the enemy. You can be holy because there is nothing too hard for God. Amen, somebody!"

Balynda found herself back on her feet and clapping her hands passionately along with many other parishioners. As she surrendered to God's will, she was again dabbing tears of joy from her eyes because she was glad to know that He cared so much and had sent another word just for her. Aunt Ida's prophecy had been a warning, and now God was reminding her that she belonged to Him. She did not have to cater to the lusts of her flesh, but God would make a way for her to resist the temptations she was facing. She just needed to trust in and depend on God. *Now that is some real good news*, she said to herself as she thanked God for not giving up on her in spite of her faults.

## ⁕ Chapter Fifteen

Monday morning Balynda met with Frank to discuss her grievance against Amy. Frank was most encouraging as he advised her that she was right to take a stand against workplace bullying. He had received many complaints about Amy, but no one wanted to act against her. He told her to first make sure Leslie, Max, and Nicole would be willing to be named in the grievance as witnesses. He also advised that without them, it would be her word against Amy's.

Before leaving for lunch, Balynda stopped by the desks of Leslie, Nicole, and Max. They all readily expressed a desire to help her however they could. She called Frank to tell him to include them in the grievance as they were all on board. She felt a sense of accomplishment knowing Frank would be filing the grievance later that day.

Balynda hurried to her car to meet Frances and Lisa for lunch. They planned to meet at a seafood restaurant in The Flats and she knew she had to get in and out so she could return to the office on time. She found a great spot within a short walking distance from the Oyster Bar. The Flats was one of Balynda's favorite places to hang out in Cleveland as it had a wide variety of excellent restaurants to choose from, exciting entertainment, and beautiful views of the Cuyahoga River. She would go there just to walk around sometimes as it had the feel of being on vacation somewhere distant.

When Balynda arrived, Lisa and Frances had already secured a table. The ladies embraced and exchanged pleasantries.

"Girl, you look good!" Frances said to Balynda. "Something or somebody got you glowing," she said with an exaggerated blink and smirk.

"I have been feeling much better today, actually," Balynda confirmed. "But it has nothing to do with Dion, or even Zeke for that matter! I know that is what you are insinuating," she laughed.

"I am filing my grievance against Amy today, so I am glad about that. She needs to know that type of behavior in the workplace is unacceptable. The union dude told me that as per my agency employee handbook, it is a violation of my rights to be berated and embarrassed in front of other employees like that. I knew it didn't feel right, but I am glad we have legal support."

"Um yeah!" Lisa added. "She trippin'." Thank God you all have union protection there. We don't at my job in the private sector."

"Well, the good thing is that you have witnesses," said Frances. "Didn't you say that Nicole from S.I.S witnessed everything?"

"Yep," Balynda replied as she took a sip of her freshly poured water. Before taking their drink orders, the waitress had come by and placed a refreshing-looking carafe full of water, lime, and lemons on the table.

"I have Nicole, my good friend, Leslie, and my buddy who sits right across from me, Max," Balynda continued. "I'm really only asking for an apology in front of those who heard her. I'm sure some sensitivity training would not hurt either."

"Right. That's the least she can do, I am sure. So, what else is going on with you? How are you and Zeke?" Lisa inquired.

The waitress returned to take their orders. The trio agreed to share a dozen chargrilled oysters as an appetizer. Balynda ordered the special, grilled tuna steak with tempura green beans and honey roasted sweet potatoes.

"I'll tell you," Balynda began. I don't think this marriage is going to survive. I think Zeke is up to his cheating again, and I just can't do it anymore. The other night he did not come in from work until almost 10:00 p.m. after leaving the house at 7:00 a.m. That is just crazy to me."

"Oh!" blurted Lisa. "Was that Thursday night?"

"Uh, yes, yes it was. Why?" Balynda questioned.

"Didn't Kim call you? She said she saw Zeke out the other

night, I do believe it was Thursday. She said he was clearly having a business meeting although they were all still having a good time. She said it was a bunch of dudes in suits looking good," Lisa laughed.

"She said she didn't approach Zeke because she was still mad at him about Cindi, so Zeke probably didn't even see her. At Adega, right?"

Balynda instantly felt horrible for not believing Zeke. She was still in disbelief as she muttered, "Yeah, that's where he said they were."

"Okay," said Lisa, "You were wrong on that one. So, what else has he done since Cindi that makes you want to end your marriage?"

"Well, nothing really. I just—"

"You just want to make it easy for the clean-up woman then, huh?" Lisa interrupted. "I mean, look Balynda, you have stuck it out with Zeke for years. Why now? What about the kids? What about all you two have acquired together? That should account for something. I know he has hurt you over and over, but what if, what if he gets it now? What if he has truly changed? Are you going to throw all that away? Along with a good man that you helped shape?"

Before Balynda could respond, Frances interjected.

"Now, hold up now. Some women tolerate zero cheating. One strike and you are out! So, why should she stay with a man who has made empty promises to her over and over again? She deserves better, but it is not my call. Just know, Balynda, that I am here for you whatever you decide to do, no matter what."

"I'm here for her too, of course. Y'all know how pissed off I was when I heard about Cindi. But I just want you to consider everything before you make such a big decision. I'm saying, you have stayed this long and now Zeke seems to be on the right track. Why would you leave now? Oh!" Lisa shouted as if a light bulb went off in her head. "There must be someone else!"

"Dang Detective Parks!" Balynda responded. "There kind of is but that is not the reason. Well, not directly, I guess. Well, sort of, kind of. I mean, perhaps he has helped me see that I deserve better, but the reason I may leave is because I am just tired of worrying about if and when Zeke will cheat on me again. That has just, just gotten really old."

"I can dig it," Lisa said. "Well, from someone who has been married twice, let me just say this, and I will get off my soapbox. Don't let your infidelity be part of the demise of your marriage. I don't know what all you have done with this dude, but take it from me, even if you get a divorce, you want to be able to say that you didn't cheat and that you did everything you could to keep your marriage together. And I know you love the Lord. Even though God allows for divorce in His permissive will when adultery has occurred, and we know Zeke has given you reason after reason to leave, cheat, and what have you—do the right thing. Don't let it be said that you were at fault. That will help you in court, in your relationship with God, and as you move forward with your life, whatever path you choose to take."

Lisa had said a mouthful and Balynda received all that she said. "I hear you."

"Well, let's get ready to dive into these oysters," Frances said as the appetizer arrived. The ladies eagerly dove into their meal forgetting any care in the world.

~ ~ ~ ~ ~

The next day, Dion and Balynda had planned to have dinner at his place around 7:00 p.m. She already knew Zeke was going to be working late that evening, and she had Desmond lined up to keep an eye on May. On her way home, she had picked dinner up for them from a neighborhood Italian restaurant around the corner from their house. She had everything ready for her evening with Dion except for her mind. She knew that going to his house was wrong, let alone what they had planned. As strongly as she wrestled to do the right thing, her desire was to fulfill her fleshly yearning. Even while she went back and forth in her mind as to what to do, her actions in moving forth with the plan revealed a person with a made-up mind.

She found herself telling lies already. "I'm just going to hang out with Ms. Frances" and "We are just going to chill at her house."

Balynda kissed the kids goodbye and headed toward Dion's condo in downtown Cleveland. She got on I-90 West and as she looked over at Lake Erie, thought fondly about her walk with Dion. In just a short period of time, he had captured her attention such that she was on the verge of doing something she had never done. She began to put what she was about to do in perspective. She was planning to break her marriage vows. She was anticipating sharing with Dion something that had been exclusively Zeke's since they rekindled their relationship after college — her body. Then she audibly heard God say, "It is not your body." The voice was so clear and vivid that Balynda actually looked around to see where it could have come from. Nothing more needed to be said, nor was anything else said. She immediately took the next exit off the interstate and made her way back home.

"I hear You, Lord, and I thank You." Tears flowed down her face. "I don't know what I'm going to do, but I know what I am not going to do, and I know that I will trust You."

She decided to stop by the lake on her way back home. She walked around enjoying the fresh air, the rippling waves, and watching the families play on the beach. She texted Dion and told him she wasn't coming and that she would call him another time to discuss. As she walked, she prayed and talked to the Lord. She knew that she still had battles to fight, but instead of worrying, she relished this victory. She had obeyed God's voice and in doing so, denied her lusts of the flesh. She knew she didn't always get it 100 percent right, but she did know that God forgave her and had given her another chance.

# ❧ Chapter Sixteen

Two weeks later, Balynda repeatedly checked the time to make sure she was not late to meet Frank. They had a meeting with the assistant director to discuss her grievance. Frank was told that the agency had been conducting a fact-finding investigation for the last couple of weeks to probe into Balynda's allegations. She was anxious to hear what they had decided regarding the incident and was also looking forward to putting it behind her. Most importantly, she wanted Amy to know that she would not be bullied and, hopefully, prevent her from treating anyone else in such a manner.

"Are you ready?" Frank asked as he greeted Balynda outside of Odessa Thomas' office.

"Yes," Balynda affirmed, wiping her moist palms on her skirt. "I'm ready."

"Good. Just let me do the talking unless you are asked a direct question. I am not sure what she is going to tell us, but just follow my lead."

Balynda was glad Frank was there with her and in her corner. Frank had been fighting for the rights of employees for years and certainly knew his stuff. It was rumored that he had a photographic memory and knew the employee handbook and union and management agreements from front to back. He was magnificently dressed, and Balynda felt empowered having him represent her.

"Well, let's do it," Frank said stated as he knocked on Odessa's door.

"Come on in," Odessa responded from behind the door. "Hey, Frank and Balynda. Please have a seat." They exchanged a few pleasantries then Odessa began the meeting.

"Well, I have, of course, reviewed your grievance. I personally interviewed all three of the witnesses you listed, and I must tell you, they all said they did not hear anything."

"What!" Balynda gasped, "You are kidding me! They, they were right there. They even encouraged me to file the grievance and agreed that I could include them."

"That's crazy," Frank added.

"Listen," Odessa stated, "I'm going to be honest with you. I do believe that something happened. I don't believe that either one of you would file this grievance frivolously. But without them, you no longer have a way to prove it. It would be your word against Amy's. I am telling you now, it may not be worth the battle."

Balynda felt like a sword had been stuck in her back. She had been betrayed by some of her closest coworkers.

"Are you telling me that Max, who sits across from me, said he didn't hear anything?" Balynda inquired.

"Max, Nicole, and Leslie all said they did not hear Amy raise her voice at you or do anything that could have created a hostile work environment," Odessa added.

Balynda felt a lump growing in her throat and anger simmering in her blood. She sat quietly for the remainder of the meeting attempting to keep her emotions at bay.

"So, as I was saying," continued Odessa, "I personally would advise you to withdraw your grievance. Quite frankly, it's not going to go anywhere at this point. Nothing is going to happen to Amy. What would you like to do?"

"This is just ridiculous," Frank stated. "I mean, they all lied to you. There is nothing you can do about that?"

"The question is, 'Is this a battle you all are willing to fight?' You have a right to keep your grievance going, but at what cost? Will you even be able to prove a wrong has been done? At the end of the day, if all you are really seeking is an apology, would it really even be sincere?"

Frank looked at Balynda to see what she wanted to do. She responded by sliding down some in her chair and shrugging her shoulders in a "whatever" gesture. "All right, we will withdraw our grievance. It is my hope that Amy will be reminded to be more respectful of the rights of employees here. This should not happen again."

"Oh, we have had a conversation. Well, thank you both, and have a good rest of your day," Odessa said, rising to her feet.

"Thank you," Balynda and Frank said simultaneously.

"Are you okay?" Frank asked Balynda once they were in the hallway.

"I can't believe this. This makes no sense to me. Why would they agree to be listed in the grievance as witnesses then turn around and lie? They were basically witnesses for Amy. I am just too through!"

"Yeah, it is amazing how afraid people are to stand up to management around here. I don't get it. But these are your friends, or so you thought."

"Right, or so I thought. Anyway, thank you so much for everything. Please keep me posted if you hear anything else."

"No problem," Frank said, heading toward his office. "You just keep your head up."

"Yeah," Balynda barely uttered. She went to the ladies' room to check her appearance. She really wanted to leave work for the day but knew she had hearings that afternoon. She was also trying to conserve her leave so, she opted to stick it out. Returning to her desk she made a point to not even look in Max's direction. She also intentionally avoided any interaction with Nicole and

Leslie which she realized was easy to do as they did not reach out to her either. As she thought back, she had been the one initiating contact with the three most recently as they must have figured she would soon find out about their betrayal. Thus, they stayed away as did she.

~ ~ ~ ~ ~

It was still summer in Cleveland, but the heat began to lessen as fall was approaching. Late August often proved to be the best weather to Balynda as it was still warm outside but not scorching hot. The breeze was light and faithful just as she liked it, and she made a point to be outside as much as possible during that time of year. Now that she had removed herself from her usual lunch buddies, she spent her lunch breaks walking around areas nearby her office or even taking walks in The Flats or along Lake Erie. She found her walks to be beneficial to her body, mind, and soul. Her new lunch routine gave her the opportunity to hear from God, clear her mind, and build her physique. It had now become a habit and Balynda wondered what she would do during her lunch break when the snow hit. She continued to keep her distance from Max, Leslie, and Nicole because she had nothing to say to them. Dion accepted her decision to slow down their friendship. He said he respected her even more for her decision to do the right thing. While they missed spending time together, they both acknowledged that it was for the best.

In addition to walking and exercising more, Balynda resumed studying her Bible and attending church more regularly. She even began to attend Bible study and joined the Social Justice Ministry. She made every effort to spend her time wisely and engage in positive activities. She planned the August S.I.S outing which included attending a festival followed by dinner at Blue Point Grille and then dessert at the Chocolate Bar. As promised, all the moms with daughters allowed them to join the festivities. May had such an amazing time that she begged Balynda to allow the young girls to come again the following month.

Balynda was hoping Nicole did not show up because she did not want May and the other daughters to see any possible drama. Balynda was not surprised to see that Nicole did not attend and was relieved she did not come. Nicole was wise for not coming as Frances and Lisa were ready to tell her a thing or two if she dared to make an appearance.

Balynda had now joined the Association of Diabetes Care and Education Specialists (ADCES), had completed two diabetes certifications, and was working on her third. Since she was making changes in her own life, she found the lifestyle coach training to be the most timely and beneficial to what she desired to accomplish. She had recently attended a health care job fair and received lots of useful information for her quest to become a certified diabetes educator.

By stopping at the Cleveland State University table, she learned that with her master's degree in social work, she met the discipline requirements to enter the standard pathway to certification as a diabetes educator. Since she also met the two years of professional practice experience in her discipline, her next focus was to obtain a minimum of 1,000 hours providing diabetes education before she could even sit for the examination.

Balynda knew that would be no easy task if she was still going to work full-time, but she was up for the challenge. She had a renewed excitement as she worked towards her career goal, and for her, there was no turning back. Zeke continued to press the issue of marital counseling as he knew she had finally become fed up with his years of unfaithfulness. While Balynda was a proponent of counseling, in her case, she did not believe there was anything the counselor could tell her that would make her change her mind about Zeke. She was simply waiting on a clear Word from the Lord as to what she should do. While many whom she confided in would remind her that God already told us in the Bible that He hates divorce, she couldn't wrap her mind around the belief that God expected her to stay in a marriage that caused her so much pain.

# Chapter Seventeen

This year, fall not only brought a turn in the seasons but change for Balynda Brown as well. Balynda kept thinking about Dion as she prepared for work in the morning. She was taking way too long deciding what to wear as her mind displayed various scenarios of how she would interact with him. This would be her first-time seeing Dion in over a month. She had not seen him since their lunch date at the lake. Although he had sent her respectful text messages every now and then to check on her, she no longer initiated contact. She was truly focused on living in a way that was pleasing in God's sight and trying to avoid all distractions.

The final hearing for the Smith case was set for this morning so she was planning to go straight to court and to the office afterward. She knew that unless Sam took their case first, she would be sitting around waiting all morning. Part of her wanted to look extra cute for Dion but she quickly cast that thought down and opted to be her usual casual but professional self. Since it was already getting nippy outside, she paired her most prized pair of camel brown boots with a khaki skirt and a burnt orange sweater. She topped it all off with a beautiful scarf that Zeke brought back for her from his trip to India. It stunningly displayed all the colors of fall and harmonized her entire outfit.

The start of fall used to make Balynda begin an early dread of winter. As she drove to court, she marveled at how much she was looking forward to each new day, regardless of the weather. She attributed her newfound appreciation to her renewed walk with God and the realization that true joy was not contingent upon fleeting circumstances. She arrived early to Judge O'Reilly's courtroom, and not seeing anyone else on her case, took a seat at the front of his waiting area. Sam was not at the check-in window, so she figured she would let him know she was there when he reappeared.

As she looked over her notes on the Smith case, she was pleased that things were looking very promising for Zakiya and Brian Jr. All the parties agreed that temporary custody should stay with the agency since Lena was working but had not yet completed her case plan. Lena preferred that over legal custody being granted to Mrs. Jackie Smith, Brian, Sr's mother, but the kids would continue their placement with Mrs. Smith and her husband as they had been since the end of July. The placement was going great, and the GAL had submitted a glowing report supporting continued care in their current home, still, Lena was counting the days until she could get her babies back.

When Balynda looked up, she saw Lena and her attorney, Tom Stewart, checking in with Sam. She was able to catch Sam's eye and gave him a wave and a smile. Although she was hesitant to talk to Lena, she knew she was required to do so. She got up and began to make her way toward Lena and Tom. Before Balynda could open her mouth, Lena blurted, "Hi Balynda! I apologize I was being so difficult last time. Girl, you know I was using then. But I am clean now! Almost six months clean!"

Lena was so excited, and it was clear she wanted to give Balynda a gigantic hug. Although Balynda was taken aback by Lena's friendliness, she opted to embrace her as she was truly happy for Lena's progress. "I'm so proud of you, Lena! You keep this up, you should be able to get your kids back in no time!"

"I know! But for now, I am fine with the kids staying with Mrs. Smith. She has been taking good care of them, and they are happy there. My visits are going well, and I am working hard on my case plan."

"Yes, you are. I see you have been job hunting and are still living at Helping Hand in the recovery program. Everything is falling into place for you. Now, I know that Brian Sr. has to do a little time for the weapons charge. When he gets out—"

"I know, I know. Stay away from him."

"Well, I'm not even saying all that. I mean, you do have two kids with him, and they are staying with his mother. I'm saying, don't let him get you off course. Put in your mind how you want to live your life and what is best for you and your children. Then don't let anybody, I mean nobody, get you off track."

"I got you. I'm going to do it this time. I have to. I feel like my time is running out."

"It just may be. You are certainly not getting any younger," Balynda chuckled. "You have put yourself, your body, your kids, and your family through enough. Try something different this time."

"You mean like, try Jesus?" Lena questioned with a smile.

"You said it, I didn't. But yes, that is exactly what I mean. God will give you a new lease on life and things you believed were impossible, you will now see are possible."

The ladies exchanged smiles and embraced again. Balynda looked around and saw that all the parties to the case were present: Mr. and Mrs. Smith, Ms. Young, and Dion.

"Looks like everyone is here. Let me go touch base with everyone and make sure we are all on the same page," Balynda said as she walked away from Lena. She stopped and talked with Ms. Young and the Smiths, and then made her way to Dion.

"Hello Attorney Jiffries," Balynda said cheerfully.

"Well, hello Mrs. Brown. Aren't we in good spirits today? It is good seeing you so joyful. How have you been?"

"I have been doing great, thank you. I'm making positive changes in my life, and I have no complaints. Plus, this case has worked out perfectly, well, except for your client having to do some time. But otherwise, all is well."

"Yeah well, I got it down to about as far as I could considering his record. He should be out in a few months. I really think he gets it this time. He has really shown that this time will hopefully, prayerfully, be his last. Look, I am honestly proud of you. If you are happy, I am happy, with me in your life or not. What we were moving toward doing wasn't right, and I knew that. So hey, I'm good. And I'm here if you ever need a friend. To me, our friendship was, or rather, is special. So, I'll always be here for you."

Dion's words touched Balynda's heart and meant so much to her. She agreed that they were friends before anything, and she cherished that relationship. However, spending time with Dion would be too great a temptation, and she had grown from that place. Before Balynda could respond to Dion, Sam called their case, and all the parties began to move toward the courtroom. As Balynda began to make her way into the courtroom for the hearing, she perceived the words of Isaiah 43:19 taking root in her soul. God was doing a new thing in her life. It was springing forth and making a way in the wilderness and rivers in the desert.

~ ~ ~ ~ ~

Balynda arrived at the agency around noon. She had taken an early walk around the lake during her lunchtime since the case did not take all morning. After the Smith matter, she took care of a few things at juvenile court, then made her way to her usual walking location. Dion hinted at having lunch together, but she told him about her routine lunch plans that she enjoyed doing solo. Dion of course understood without any pushback, and they agreed to keep in touch.

As Balynda logged on to her computer, she looked over at Max. She still had not spoken to him since her meeting with Odessa and Frank. Her anger had subsided over time, yet she still could not believe that she had been betrayed by her friends.  As she opened Outlook, it came to her mind how Jesus must have felt when He was betrayed by Judas. He had traveled with Judas, taught Judas, and broken bread with him. Her spirit grew unsettled as she pondered about how she had not forgiven her coworkers. If she was going to continue to grow in her relationship with God, she would have to let go of her hurt. She crafted an email to Leslie, Max, and Nicole.

*Good afternoon,*

*I hope you all have been well. In an effort to move past the hurt, I am forgiving you. Please understand that your actions really upset me, which demonstrated to me how important you are to me. While forgiveness does require that I no longer hold your past actions against you, it does not require that I lack wisdom as we move forward.*

*Be blessed,*

*Balynda*

She read the email a couple of times and then pressed send.

She debated removing the last sentence but genuinely believed that forgiving someone did not require continuously putting herself in the same position to be hurt repeatedly. God loved her too much for that, and she wanted them to recognize that she deserved better.

~ ~ ~ ~ ~

When Balynda arrived home from work that evening, May was at gymnastics practice and Desmond had basketball tryouts. Zeke always arrived home after she did, so she knew not to expect him. Balynda grabbed her mail and headed to her bedroom to unwind. As she sorted through the mail, she saw a letter addressed to her from the Cleveland Clinic.

"Ooh!"

Excited, she hoped they said yes to an internship in their diabetes center. As one of the nation's top hospitals, she knew that getting her foot in the door at the Cleveland Clinic would be a fantastic way to start her new career.

"Yes!"

They wanted to begin her diabetes education training on Monday, October 3, 2016. They were aware that she was still working full-time, so her hours were from 5:00 p.m. to 8:00 p.m. during the week and 8:00 a.m. to 12:00 p.m. on Saturdays. This schedule made it achievable to obtain her goal of 1000 hours in a year. She got down on her knees and thanked God for everything going on in her life. She had been in some dark valleys, but God was bringing her into the marvelous light. As she praised and worshipped God, she knew that the battle was not over.

As with her coworkers, God told her to forgive Zeke. This forgiveness enabled her to no longer bind Zeke to his past infidelities. Through God, she was able to let that go, and in turn, free herself. This forgiveness gave her space to exercise wisdom and guard her heart. She concluded her prayer, wiped her face, and walked confidently towards the hallway. As she walked, she glanced at the family pictures on the wall that they took a couple of years ago. She continued her walk undeterred, unwavering, and uninhibited. Her mind went to Abraham, whom God told to leave his homeland for a destination of which he was not aware. His faith empowered her as she went to her hallway closet and removed her suitcase.